Neptune Princess

by Ingrid Tomey

Bradbury Press/New York

Maxwell Macmillan Canada/Toronto
Maxwell Macmillan International
New York/Oxford/Singapore/Sydney

For Georgena

Bradbury Press
Macmillan Publishing Company
866 Third Avenue
New York, NY 10022

Maxwell Macmillan Canada, Inc.
1200 Eglinton Avenue East
Suite 200
Don Mills, Ontario M3C 3N1

Macmillan Publishing Company is part of the Maxwell Communication Group of Companies.

First edition
Printed and bound in the United States of America
10 9 8 7 6 5 4 3 2 1

Library of Congress Cataloging-in-Publication Data
Tomey, Ingrid.
    Neptune princess / Ingrid Tomey.—1st ed.
        p.   cm.
    Summary: A broken leg means ten-year-old Poppy won't compete in the swimming events to be "Neptune Princess," but another challenge comes her way that summer that is much more important.
    ISBN 0-02-789403-7
    [1. Legs—Fracture—Fiction.]   I. Title.
PZ7.T5844Ne   1992   91-30502
[Fic]—dc20

Contents

1

The Curse

The beginning of the worst summer of her life started when Poppy fell off the roof. She knew she shouldn't have been spying on Cootie. She knew that climbing on the roof was forbidden by both her father and her mother. And she knew it was a long way down from her upstairs bedroom window to the ground. But she did it. And she fell screaming through the dark summer night and landed with a terrible, horrible thump.

Poppy's mother was the first one out of the house. She came flying out the backdoor in her blue-and-white striped pajamas. She gasped when she spotted Poppy lying still as a rag doll in her silver-star jeans under the maple tree. Then she yelled. "Poppy! Are you hurt?"

Poppy could hear her mother yelling. She could even smell the cherry lotion her mother put on her face before she went to bed. But she couldn't say a word.

"Don't move," her mother said, pushing her head back down. "Tiz," she yelled. Poppy's brother's name was really Curtis but everyone called him Tiz. "Tiz!" she yelled again, and Poppy heard the backdoor slam.

"Poppy fell out of the tree," her mother yelled at Tiz. Then she leaned over Poppy. "Can you talk now?"

Poppy opened her eyes and looked into her mother's eyes behind her rosy glasses. She wanted to say that she fell off the roof, not out of a tree. But she didn't have enough breath.

"My leg," she whimpered.

"Oh, oh," Tiz said. He knelt down beside Poppy and examined her twisted leg. Then he shook his head. "I think it's broken, Pop."

Her mom drove them to Sparrow Hospital Emergency and two men came running out to the car with a wheelchair. By that time her leg hurt so much that she didn't care who saw her crying. "My leg," she sobbed.

Poppy's mother held her hand and ran alongside the wheelchair in the flowered skirt she had put on. Underneath, Poppy could still see the blue-and-white legs of her pajamas hanging out, but she didn't care if her mother looked like a crazy lady. All she could think about was her leg.

"I'll bet they slap a cast on you," Tiz said after they had put Poppy into a bed behind a white curtain.

"We won't know until the doctor comes," her mother said, squeezing Poppy's hand.

A nurse came behind the curtain with a needle. She smiled at Poppy. "This will take the pain away and make you drowsy."

After the shot another nurse came around the curtain with a pair of scissors. "Hi, Sugar," she said, patting Poppy's hand. "I'm going to have to cut you out of those jeans."

Poppy blinked. She tried to sit up. She knew the nurse was joking. Grown-ups didn't cut up perfectly good clothes, and her silver star jeans were brand-new. Her father had brought them back from London in the spring. When the nurse opened the scissors at the right leg of her jeans, Poppy screamed, "No-ooo-oo." She tried to move her leg, but the pain was so sharp that she started to cry again.

"I'm sorry, Sugar," the nurse soothed, taking the first cut.

Snip snip snip. Poppy watched tearfully as the scissors chewed a long, ugly gash up her jeans leg. In less than a minute, the bright blue leg with its row of silver stars lay against the hospital sheet like one of her mother's dusting rags. Poppy reached down and picked it up. She draped the denim over her face and she left it there when somebody wheeled her bed down to X ray.

"Who is this under the blue cloth?" she heard a woman's joking voice say.

"I don't think she wants to talk right now," her mother answered.

She was glad the cloth hid her face. Tears continued to trickle the entire time they were taking X-ray pictures. She felt the points of the stars resting against her cheeks, on her right eyebrow and her lips, and she thought of her father going into a store looking for the most beautiful blue jeans in London. He would be dashed, she was sure of it, when he saw what had happened to her silver star jeans.

Poppy felt herself being wheeled out of the room and down the hallway. The wheels of the bed clicked along the tile and she could feel herself jiggling like a Jell-O cube. She was starting to feel droopy like she got at the drive-in movie with her mom and dad. She could hardly keep her eyes open. Close by, she heard her mother talking to a man. Maybe her father had rushed back from Turkey or China or wherever he was and he was standing there with a big hug just for her. Poppy pulled off the blue cloth. "Dad, is that you?"

The man who was standing there didn't have her father's round, rosy face or his fuzzy red mustache. He didn't have any mustache at all and his face was skinny. So were his eyes. And the top of his head was shiny.

"I'm Dr. Rosenberg," he said, holding out his hand.

Poppy knew it was silly, but she felt crushed when Dr. Rosenberg wasn't her father. "What are you going to do to me?" she asked gloomily.

He smiled and patted her hand. "I'm going to set your leg."

Poppy stared at him. "Where are you going to set it?" She pictured him wrapping up her leg and putting it in one of the white metal cupboards against the wall.

Now he smiled so broadly that his little raisin eyes almost shut. "You've broken the tibia, Poppy—the biggest bone in your leg. So I'm

6

going to set it straight. Then I'll put your leg in a cast so it will stay in place until it heals."

"It's broken?" she repeated. She put the blue cloth over her face and started to cry again.

"Don't cry, Pumpkin," her mother said. "Skillions of people break their legs."

"You'll be good as new in eight or nine weeks," Dr. Rosenberg said.

"I brought you a candy bar," Tiz said, holding something chocolate-smelling under her nose.

But Poppy was thinking about the curse Cootie had put on her for spying—about that one instant when Cootie had looked up at her with her mean little face twisted like a Halloween mask. That was the moment Poppy went off the roof. Because of Cootie she was going to miss being Neptune Princess, the biggest honor of her life.

2

~~~~~~

Poppy's Broken Stem

Poppy was running, running, running across a meadow of wildflowers. The sun was shining and it danced down over her yellow hair and shoulders all the way to her bare feet. She was leaping like a deer over daisies and buttercups, over black-eyed Susans. Now she was leaping over bushes and rocks. Ahead of her was a huge gray boulder, higher than a house. Her feet pounded against the warm earth, building up speed. She jumped, rising up off the ground like a Ping-Pong ball. Suddenly, a tiny white claw reached out from under the boulder, grabbing her ankle, and Poppy went tumbling headfirst over the boulder and down, down, down, like a rag doll into dark, empty space. Falling, falling, falling. Above her she could hear the wicked cackling of Cootie.

Poppy woke with a start from the frightening dream. She wanted to sit up on the sofa, but she couldn't move. The pain in her leg made her moan and shut her eyes again. She reached under the sheet and touched the hard, bumpy log that started just below her underpants. She ran her hand down it as far as she could to where her knee should have been. But where was her knee? She wanted to rub the long, terrible ache that she felt inside the cast. What if they had cut her leg off, just like Cootie's, and they put a cast on to make her think she still had a leg? She tried to pull up her left foot so she could sit up, but even that was impossible. Her right leg hurt so badly she wanted to scream, but she didn't have the energy. So she just moaned and slumped back on the pillow.

But the little moan brought her mother from the kitchen. "Pop, are you okay?"

Poppy pointed. "My leg."

"Oh, Sweetie, it hurts, doesn't it?"

"Did the doctor cut it off?" Poppy looked at her mother's eyes behind the glasses. She knew her eyes would tell the truth.

"Cut it off?" Her mother looked like she was going to laugh but she didn't. She put her arms around Poppy and smoothed her straggly bangs. "Of course the doctor didn't cut off your leg, Sweetie. Look down there at the end of your cast. What do you see?"

Poppy looked down the long white log. "Oh," she said, feeling stupid. "Toes." She wiggled them back and forth. "Ouch." Even that hurt.

"Just lie still," her mother said, lowering her back onto the pillow. "This week we'll be your slaves. We'll bring you food and books and anything your little heart desires. Tiz has already brought your things from upstairs—let's see, hairbrush, toothbrush, radio, clothes." She pursed her lips. "We're going to have to do something about your clothes."

Poppy had been lying there with her eyes shut, only half listening. Now she opened her eyes and looked down at the baggy blue T-shirt she was wearing. It was Tiz's. "Where are my silver star jeans?" she asked. "The part I was still wearing?"

Her mother sighed and pushed her glasses up with her index finger. "I'm sorry, Pop, but they had to go. We couldn't pull them down over your cast after we got you to bed last night."

"My silver star jeans? You cut them to shreds?"

Her mother nodded sadly.

"Where are they?" Poppy said, painfully lifting herself from the pillow. "I want them."

"Poppy, you're being silly. There's no way I can piece them together."

Tears sprang to her eyes. "Daddy bought

those for me. I'm going to keep them forever and ever."

Her mother shook her head as if Poppy were a hopeless case. Then she got up and went over to the green duck wastebasket at the end of the sofa. She lifted out two pieces of star-covered denim, and shook them to dislodge a couple of potato chips. "They're kind of grubby."

"No, they're not," Poppy said, reaching for them. She knew she sounded bratty, but she didn't care. She hugged the pieces, comforted by having a reminder of her father next to her heart. "When's Daddy coming home? Does he know about my broken leg?"

Her mother nodded. "I called him last night and he feels terrible."

"Is he going to fly home from Istanbul?" Poppy asked, picturing her father, running with his suitcases to catch a taxi. "Step on it," he would shout. "My daughter has a broken leg."

"Spain," her mother said. "He's in Spain

and he can't leave for at least two weeks, but he sends his love."

"Oh, poo," Poppy said. Her father always sent his love even when she was one hundred percent healthy. Gloomily, she lay back down and put the leg of her jeans over her head, feeling the cool points of the stars arranging themselves on her face. "Now what am I supposed to do?" she said, her lips quivering. The pain in her leg was as steady as a ticking clock.

"How about some pancakes?" her mother said brightly. "I'll go whip some up and we'll eat them out here on the sofa."

"I'm never going to eat again," Poppy moaned. As she lay there with the cloth over her face, Poppy thought about Cootie. Her name was really Mrs. Kootabelli and she was about a hundred years old and she lived next door. Cootie never cut her grass or trimmed her bushes. Everything had grown around her house, so you couldn't even see it anymore. And she had put broken cinder blocks around her yard to keep people out. Poppy's mother called her "a poor old soul," but Poppy and all of her friends thought she was a witch. They had heard that Cootie caught all the loose cats in the neighborhood and boiled them in a kettle out on her crumbly old barbecue pit. Every day Poppy saw smoke rising from her backyard, but her parents said Cootie was just burning trash.

Once, when she was little, Poppy sneaked over to see if Cootie was boiling cats. She had to crawl over the broken cinder blocks and through the shrubs and then duck under all the blankets that Cootie kept on her line. At first she didn't see Cootie. What she saw were dozens of little statues all over the lawn— painted squirrels and ladybugs and flamingos and Mickey and Minnie Mouse. It was like a crazy little circus. Poppy wanted to crawl around on her hands and knees and look at everything. But suddenly, Cootie was coming at her, shaking her cane, her mean face all squinched up. "You—girl," she yelled. "You come here."

In a flash, Poppy ducked under the blankets and scrambled back to her own yard. She ran in the backdoor and up the stairs, and hid in a closet. And she never went back into Cootie's backyard. But last Halloween, she and Marcie stood out on the street while Greg Piper soaped her front windows. And then last night . . . She shivered thinking about it. She had been pretending she was a spy, like Mata Hari, the famous lady spy her fourth grade teacher had told them about. Mata Hari was beautiful and dressed in glittery clothes and went behind enemy lines to spy. That was why Poppy had put on her fancy star jeans before she crawled out on the roof. She had a perfect view down into Cootie's kitchen window, and she could see her hobbling around, going from the sink to the stove to her little brown table, with a cup of tea.

What she wanted to see most of all, what she promised Marcie and Greg she would report on, was Cootie's wooden leg. She wanted to see Cootie take off her wooden leg. But she just sat there like a boring housewife, drinking her tea. Poppy was about to give up and climb back in her bedroom window when Cootie looked up. She looked up from her teacup to just exactly where Poppy was sitting, in one flash. And when she saw Poppy sitting there on the roof, spying on her, she squinched up her face and pointed a skinny little finger right at her. That was the curse. That was the moment Poppy's feet slid out from under her and she went tumbling over the side of the house, through the air, and into a broken heap under the tree.

Now Poppy shivered, feeling the weight of Cootie's curse. Her leg throbbed. Her whole body ached.

"Here we go," her mother said, coming back into the living room. "Look at this," she said, taking the cloth off Poppy's face.

On the tray was a big stack of pancakes and next to it was a white glass pitcher of runny strawberries—Poppy's favorite. Also on the tray was a blue china vase holding two big red flowers.

"Poppies," Poppy said, smiling for the first time that morning.

"They just bloomed," her mother said, lifting the vase off the tray. "Aren't they gorgeous?" And then she said what she said every year when the poppies bloomed. "In Flanders Field, the poppies blow . . ."

"Beside the crosses row on row," Poppy finished for her. Poppy's mother was a poet and she was always spouting poetry. Poetry was the reason she gave Poppy her name. So she would be a Poppy Field, like the poppy field in the poem.

Poppy liked it when people caught on to her name. "Poppy Field?" they would say, and then they would smile. "You mean like a field of poppies?" And she could see them picturing hundreds and hundreds of red poppies waving in the sunshine. Her mother said her name was very picturesque, meaning it made a picture in your mind. Poppy was glad to have a picturesque name.

"Are you hungry?" her mother asked, tucking a pink napkin into the neck of Tiz's T-shirt.

"Maybe I could eat a little bit," Poppy said, wincing as she sat up.

Her mother lifted a glass of orange juice to Poppy's lips. Poppy had never been so tired and so achey. And she had never had a curse on her before. It was comforting to have her mother hovering over her with a worried expression. Poppy finished the orange juice in tiny sips, and then she took the plate of pancakes from her mother. "More," she said, holding the plate while her mother poured runny strawberries over it. She didn't say "enough" until the strawberries reached her thumb. Her mother stood over her while she ate, and asked if she wanted another pillow behind her back and if she wanted more pancakes.

"Poor Poppy," she said as Poppy handed her the plate back. "Poor little Poppy Field."

It made Poppy feel important, being waited on like that, so when her mother piled up everything on the tray and started back to the kitchen, Poppy sat up. "Where are you going?"

"I have two poems to finish," her mother said, already on her way to the kitchen. She wrote six poems a week for two newspapers, plus she had a business called Poems by Prue (short for Prudence). People hired her to write poems for their sweethearts or their new babies or for someone's birthday.

"Write them out here," Poppy pleaded. "I'll be quiet."

"Can't," her mother called back. "I'm plugged in out here." She meant her electric typewriter.

"Oh please, oh please, oh please," Poppy hollered. To her amazement, her mother came back into the room. She was carrying a red marker. She bent over Poppy's cast, in her thinking posture, her hand on her forehead.

"What are you doing?"

"I'm going to be the first person to sign your cast," she said. And with that she dropped to her knees and started writing in neat little red letters from the middle of the cast down toward Poppy's ankle. When she finished, she got up, snapped the cap back on the marker, and went back to the kitchen.

Poppy twisted her head sideways to read what her mother had written:

This is Poppy's broken stem—
In time our flower will bloom again.

Poppy sighed and flopped back on the pillow. If only she could bloom in time for Neptune Carnival, the biggest event of the year. Every kid at her beach competed for red, white, and blue ribbons, but the biggest honor went to the Neptune Princess or Neptune Prince. This was the boy or girl between the ages of ten and twelve who scored the highest in all the swimming and diving events. And this was Poppy's year to win. She felt it in her bones. She had been swimming and diving since she was five years old, and she knew she was better than any other girl or boy her age. She punched her pillow. Of all summers to have a curse on her.

3

The Big Lie

While Poppy sat on the edge of the sofa, Tiz demonstrated the crutches they had picked up. The therapist had demonstrated how to walk and bend and go in and out of doors, but Poppy had been too achey and tired to try them.

"You look stupid," Poppy said impatiently, as she watched tall, skinny Tiz thump back and forth.

"Watch me," Tiz said, "and visualize yourself doing the same thing. The way these armrests cradle your pits, the way you plant the poles, lift, plant your leg, lift, plant the poles. You see the rhythm here? That's the thing. Get the rhythm down and you've got it."

Poppy felt like being a lazy lump all day. But she watched him as he crossed from the kitchen doorway to the bottom of the stairs and back, and pretty soon she imagined she was Tiz. She felt herself plant and swing, plant and swing. She even imagined the pressure of the crutches under her arms. "Okay," she said finally. "I can do it."

"Here," he said, handing over the crutches. "Let's see."

She stood on one leg and Tiz shoved the crutches under her arms. "Plant and swing," he said. "Plant and swing."

Poppy crutched her way smoothly toward the kitchen, turned around, and crutched past Tiz to the stairway and then back to Tiz.

"All ri-i-ght," he said, clapping. "Way to go, Pop. See what a little visualization can do. I use it to practice the piano when I'm in bed.

I just imagine my fingers running up and down the keyboard. If you imagine yourself doing something enough times, it's like you're actually doing it."

"It was easy," Poppy said.

"Well, you had a great instructor," he said. Then he added, "'Course, you're pretty coordinated to start with."

Poppy beamed. Tiz was a computer whiz and a great piano player, but Poppy was a far better swimmer. She could also run faster than Tiz and she could ski. Tiz couldn't even do the bunny hills. She loved it when he bragged about her to his friends. He said things like, "Sure, she can swim faster than me. But turn her over—she's got a dorsal fin."

She crutched across the living room again and Tiz said, "Hey, whose shorts are those?"

Poppy looked down at the saggy red shorts. They were all lumpy in the middle where her mom had pinned them with a safety pin. "My shorts won't fit over my cast," she said. "I have to wear yours until Mom makes me some."

"Oh, terrific. I bring all your clothes downstairs and you wear mine." He rolled his eyes, but Poppy knew he wasn't really mad. Tiz hardly ever got really mad at her. But he didn't pay much attention to her, either. That's why she was so happy he took the time to show her how to use her crutches.

"Hey," he said, looking at his watch, "I gotta run." Tiz had a summer job at their dad's office. He kept track, on the computer, of all the business machines. If a customer wanted a certain copy machine, he could look it up on the computer in one minute to see if they had it. He sat in a little office with seven old women. Poppy and her mom brought him a sack of cookies one day so they could go upstairs and see where he worked.

"Tiz, would you bring me something from upstairs? It's the globe Dad got me. It's hanging from—"

Tiz didn't wait for her to finish. He dashed up the stairs and came back down and threw it at her. "You'll have to ask Mom to hang it. See you." He slammed the door, and in a second Poppy heard his old yellow car chugging off down the street.

Poppy sat on the sofa turning the globe over and over in her hands. It wasn't a real globe like they had in Mrs. Robb's fourth grade. It was a beach ball. But it had all the countries on it and all the bodies of water just like a real globe. Her father brought it back from England and hung it from her ceiling so she could find the countries he traveled to. Finally, she found Spain, below France. It stuck out in the ocean like a duck's foot. She saw that the beach ball was getting saggy, so she unplugged it and blew into it until Spain was nice and snug again. She picked out Madrid, the capital of Spain, and she also picked out a river with an unusual name, the Guadalquivir. The Guadalquivir River. It rhymed. Because of all the poetry her mother wrote, Poppy always noticed words that rhymed. Oh Dad, so sad, by the Guadalquivir River, she thought. But her dad wasn't so sad. He wasn't even coming home early because of her broken leg.

She put the beach ball down and reached for

her crutches. All week her mother had waited on her, bringing her soup and crackers on a tray, Popsicles and grape juice. She even came in to read her poems to Poppy. One was about clothes drying on the line; another was a poem in honor of a new baby. But today she had stayed in the kitchen. Poppy knew she was sitting at the kitchen table, her fingers tapping away like little machines. When her mother was writing, she forgot all about Poppy. Sometimes she forgot to pick Poppy up from swimming practice. She would even forget to fix dinner till her father would walk into the kitchen, and say, "Prue, are we eating poems for dinner again?" Then her mother would slap her forehead and jump up and begin opening cans like crazy.

Poppy slowly crutched her way into the kitchen and, sure enough, there was her mother at the table with a million papers spread out around her. She was staring at a page in the typewriter and didn't look up until Poppy said, "Mom."

"Oh, Poppy, look at you." Her mother smiled. "Walking around here like you were born on crutches. It must be wonderful to be so athletic. How does this sound?" She poked up her glasses and peered at the sheet of typing paper. She cleared her throat.

"My daughter climbed the maple tree,
She climbed it to the top.
And when she reached the topmost branch,
She heard a little pop."

Poppy swallowed. "Ummm, is that about me?"

"No, it's about Alice in Wonderland, silly. What do you think?" her mother went on. "She started to fall, like a bird from its nest—no, too corny. She started to fall—"

"Mom, do you always have to write about me?" Poppy said, sinking into a chair and propping her cast on another chair.

"What?" Her mother looked surprised. "You love it when I write about you."

It was true. Poppy liked the attention she got when there was a poem about her in the paper. When Poppy was six, her mother wrote about Poppy pulling out her first tooth. And her first grade teacher read it to the class. When Poppy won her first Neptune Carnival ribbon, the *McGregor Beach Weekly* published her mother's poem on the first page. But this poem was a big lie. Poppy still hadn't told her mother she fell off the roof.

Poppy picked up the butter knife. "I hate this cast," she said, hitting it with the knife, even though it sent little shocks down her leg.

"You'd better make friends with it," her mother said. "You're going to have it on all summer."

"Not all summer!" Poppy said. "Eight or nine weeks."

"Well, that takes you to the middle of August," her mother said, taking the butter knife from Poppy's hand.

Glumly, Poppy ate her cereal while her mother began tapping away again.

"I want to go swimming," Poppy announced.

"I'm sure you do," her mother said, without stopping. "But you don't want to get your cast wet."

"I want to go swimming," Poppy repeated stubbornly.

Her mother stopped typing and rolled her little gray office chair over to where Poppy sat. "Let's go over the rules one more time. You can't get your cast wet or what will happen?" She looked at Poppy.

Poppy shrugged, wishing her mother would go back to typing.

"Or you'll have to go back and have a new cast put on. And you must use your crutches at all times. If you put any weight on your broken leg, you might dislocate the parts that are broken and Dr. Rosenberg will have to set it again."

"I'm never going back there," Poppy said, pushing away her cereal bowl. "I'm not going back to Dr. Rosenberg and I'm going to go swimming every day and I'm going to march upstairs and sleep in my own bed."

She leaned sideways to grab her crutches from against the counter. The crutches toppled over, striking the table and snagging the box of cereal. Cornflakes shot into the air and rained down on their heads. Poppy looked at her mother and wailed, "I wish I didn't have a leg."

Her mother came over and put her arms around Poppy. "Dr. Rosenberg said your leg would hurt for a week or two. Why don't you just be a sloth for a while? I know—you can memorize an extra poem and we'll go on a picnic Sunday."

"I can't," Poppy sniffled. "I can't think."

"Memorize the poem I'm writing about you falling out of the tree. That should be a cinch."

Poppy sighed, wishing she could tell her mother the truth. She was really beginning to hate the Big Lie.

Later in the afternoon, Poppy was back on the sofa, hitting the beach ball over her head and watching it swing back and forth from a string her mother had taped to the ceiling. Lying down, all she could see was Antarctica, and she wondered if her father ever went there. She was picturing her father dressed in a big furry parka, standing on the back of a dogsled, icicles hanging off his mustache, when the doorbell rang.

In a minute her mom came in with Poppy's best friend, Marcie, and her next-best friend, Kim. They were each carrying a present.

Poppy sat up and smiled. "Hi, you guys." She waited for them to look at her leg and say how awful it was.

Marcie was first. "Oh, my gosh," she said. "I thought it would just be a little cast, like when Stewie broke his ankle, but this is huge." Stewie was her little brother. "It looks like a— a—"

"Telephone pole," said Kim. "It must weigh a hundred pounds. Does it hurt?"

"It kills," said Poppy cheerfully. "You should have seen it the night I fell. It looked like a pretzel. It really killed then."

Marcie and Kim sat down on the floor next to the sofa and put their presents next to them. Poppy wondered what they had brought her, but she was too polite to ask.

"Did you fall from the very top of the tree?" Kim asked.

Poppy hesitated. Her mother had already gone back in the kitchen, but it didn't seem right to tell them and not her mother. "Not the very top," she said lamely.

Marcie leaned forward and whispered, "I guess you didn't get to see Cootie's you-know-what."

Poppy looked into Marcie's dark eyes, longing to tell her best friend about the horrible curse Cootie had put on her, but how could she tell her without telling her about falling off the roof?

"My father says it's a crime the way she never takes her flag down," Kim volunteered. "It's been up there so long it looks like an old gray rag."

Poppy didn't want to talk about Cootie. She wanted to talk about her leg. "Anyway, you guys, I have to walk everywhere on these things."

"Oh, rude," Kim said, wrinkling her nose.

"I tried my brother's crutches, but they were too short," Marcie said, reaching for Poppy's crutches.

"I'll show you," Poppy said, pushing herself up.

As soon as she stood up, Kim and Marcie started giggling. "Are those your father's shorts?" Marcie pointed at the red shorts.

Poppy suddenly felt stupid in Tiz's big, droopy shorts, but she forced a laugh. "They're Tiz's. Aren't they awful? My shorts won't go over my cast. I can barely even get my underpants on."

Kim doubled over. "Why don't you, why don't you wear—"

"Tiz's underwear," Marcie finished, and they both exploded into laughter.

It didn't seem that funny to Poppy. She

dropped back on the sofa, letting her crutches fall on the floor. "What did you bring me?" she asked, tired of being polite.

"Oh, here," Marcie said, handing her the gift. "My mom and I went out and bought you this as soon as we heard about your leg." Poppy opened the card. Her mother was a freak about reading the card first. "Just a little sunshine ray—Beaming a wish that you're better today." Cornball stuff. It was signed Marcie and Mrs. Donnell. Mrs. Donnell had written underneath, "So sorry about your accident. We can't have the star athlete of McGregor Beach laid up for long." The present was a sketch-book.

"My mom thought you might want to take up drawing this summer," Marcie said, "since you can't do anything else."

Kim's present was some red bath oil. "I'm not allowed to take a bath," Poppy said, "for eight or nine weeks."

"Oh, rude," Kim said, plugging her nose.

"I can take a shower with a garbage bag on my leg."

She didn't tell them that her mother had to help her wash up at night and help her into her clothes in the morning. Anyway, that was all going to end. Poppy was ready to do things for herself again. "Thanks for the presents," she said. "What do you want to do?"

"Want to go swimming?" Kim asked. Then, seeing the expression on Poppy's face, she said, "Oh, forget it."

"Hey," Marcie said suddenly. "Are you going to get your cast off for Neptune?"

Poppy shook her head. "Eight or nine weeks, the doctor said."

Marcie waved her hand across the air. "Oh, doctors always tell you it'll be longer than it is. The doctor told Stewie six weeks and he had it off in a month. I'll bet you get yours off in seven weeks."

Poppy's heart suddenly lifted like a balloon. She could still swim. She could still be Neptune Princess.

Then Kim added, "But I hope you don't."

"What!" Poppy stared at her friend.

Kim grinned. "Everyone knows you're

going to be Neptune Princess. If you swim I won't have a chance."

"Yeah," Marcie said. "Me neither."

Suddenly Poppy had a vision of herself standing on the winner's platform in her red swimsuit. On her head was the gold Neptune Princess crown with red rubies glued all over it. Everyone was cheering and her mom and Tiz were waving from the crowd. Her dad was taking hundreds of pictures of her, and Poppy was smiling as if her face would break. The crowd was chanting her name. "Poppy, Poppy, Poppy—"

"Poppy," Kim said, "can we sign your cast?" With red marker she wrote: "Roses are red, violets are blue. I'm sure glad that I'm not you."

Marcie wrote: "Get the crown ready."

4

Statue

*Poppy was having another dream. She was out-*side running in the grass again, doing somer-saults and back flips and cartwheels. Marcie was with her and Kim and a bunch of kids from her class. Poppy was doing cartwheels—seven, eight, nine of them in a row. As she was springing up from her tenth cartwheel, a creaky little voice said, "Freeze." Poppy came down hard with her feet apart, her hands over her head, and stayed that way, like a gingerbread cookie. Everyone went screaming away, but

Poppy couldn't move. She was frozen. And then she saw that she was in Cootie's backyard, and all around were the statues of little animals and birds and children. Poppy realized with horror that she had turned into one of Cootie's statues.

"It's a beautiful day for a picnic." Her mother's voice awakened her. She pulled open the living room drapes and sunlight streamed in across the blue carpeting. "What a sleepyhead you are. It's ten o'clock," her mother said, pointing at the grandfather clock that was just making its first bong.

Poppy threw her pillow on the floor and then her blankets. She lifted her left leg in the air. Then she lifted her cast. She turned around and sat up, bending over from the waist to hang her head down till her hair dragged on the floor. She wiggled her tongue back and forth in her mouth. "Lootle lootle lootle lootle."

Her mother laughed. "Poppy, what in the world are you doing?"

Poppy sat back up. "I just wanted to make sure I'm not a statue. I had this weird dream."

"What?" Her mother came and sat down beside her. Poppy's mother was fascinated by dreams. She wrote down her own dreams every morning. Sometimes she even wrote them down in the middle of the night.

"I dreamed I was doing cartwheels on the lawn and I turned into a statue."

"What kind of a statue?"

"Just like me—only I couldn't move."

"Anything else?"

"Well, a lot of my friends were jumping around with me, and Cootie"—she looked at her mother—"I mean Mrs. Kootabelli, came out of her house and said, 'Freeze.' But I was the only one who did."

"How strange," her mother said. "How interesting."

Her mother always said, "How strange, how interesting," and then tried to figure out what it meant. Poppy knew it meant that Cootie had put a curse on her, but she couldn't tell her mother this. She shivered.

Her mother bent down and hugged her. "I think it means you don't like being in a cast.

You hate not being able to jump around like you always do. Being in a cast is very difficult for whirling dervishes."

Her parents always called her a whirling dervish. It wasn't that she liked to whirl so much; she just didn't like to stand still.

"Come and have breakfast," her mother said, "and you can recite your poems."

It was Poppy's fourteenth day in a cast and things were back to normal in her house. Her mother expected her to fix her own breakfast once again, and Tiz griped if she asked him to bring anything down from her bedroom. While Poppy hobbled around getting cornflakes and milk and a bowl, she began reciting. "Little Wind," she said, "by Kate Greenaway."

"Little wind, blow on the hilltop,
Little wind, blow down the plain;
Little wind, blow up the sunshine,
Little wind, blow off the rain."

"Well, that was brief," her mother said. She handed Poppy a dollar.

Unlike her friends, Poppy didn't have regular chores. Her mother didn't care if Poppy made her bed. She said Poppy had to live in her room so how she kept it was up to her. The only allowance Poppy got was a dollar a week for memorizing a poem. It didn't matter how long the poem was, she always got a dollar. She hardly ever went over eight lines. But her mother was disappointed if she only did four, like today. "I had a tough week," Poppy said.

"Do you have another poem?" her mother asked. That was the deal. If Poppy wanted to do something special, like go on a picnic, she could memorize another poem.

"Clouds," she said, "by Christina Rosetti."

"White sheep, white sheep
On a blue hill,
When the wind stops
You all stand still.
When the wind blows
You walk away slow.
White sheep, white sheep,
Where do you go?"

"Mmmm, that's lovely," her mother said. "What is she really writing about?"

Poppy hated it when her mother asked questions about the poems. "White sheep?" she asked, looking up from her cereal.

"Not really," her mother said. "Think of the title."

"Clouds?"

"Yes, she's comparing the clouds in the sky to white sheep on a blue hill."

"Oh, yeah," Poppy said, taking a bite of toast. "Is it all right if I ask Marcie and Kim?"

"Sure," her mom said. "Do you want pickle relish in your egg salad?"

"It must be awful to sit like that," Kim said. She and Marcie and Mrs. Field were seated on one side of the picnic table and Poppy was sitting on the other side with her cast stretched out on the bench.

Poppy shrugged and bit into her sandwich. "It's okay," she said.

"Yeah, but I bet your leg gets all hot and sticky in there," she said. "Especially like now."

Poppy's leg inside her cast *was* all hot and sticky. It was itchy, too. She felt like a million little red ants were crawling up and down her broken leg. If only she could take a hose and squirt it down inside the cast, the hot, itchy, little-ant feeling would go away.

"I'm sweltering hot," said Kim. "I wish we were by the lake. Don't you wish we could go swimming?"

Poppy glared at her.

"Oh, we can do that anytime," Marcie said loyally. "But we never get to come to Wheelock Park. My parents never bring me here," she told Mrs. Field. "The last time I was here was with you and Poppy. Remember, Poppy? We climbed up the hill when the train was coming and put pennies on the track." Marcie pointed at the steep hill and they all looked up through the tangle of little bushes and wildflowers to the top.

Poppy thought about climbing that hill—how easily she and Marcie had scrambled to the top, the feel of dry dust in her nostrils, and the rushing whine of the train over the tracks. She could never climb it now, not in a million years. She turned her head and finished her sandwich.

"Hey, let's go on the merry-go-round," Marcie said. "C'mon, Poppy, we'll push you."

Poppy's spirits lifted and she reached for her crutches. Then Kim thought of something funny. "I know—we can be your crutches. Marcie, you get under one arm and I'll get under the other."

They all started laughing. "This is really going to be weird," Marcie said. "I'm too tall."

"Scrooch down," Poppy said, pushing her on the head. She put her arms around her two friends and they all started laughing.

"You girls be very careful," her mother said. "Don't let her fall."

"We're not girls, we're crutches," Kim said. "One and a two and a crutch, crutch, crutch."

They started off unsteadily in the direction of the merry-go-round. Marcie and Kim chanted, "Crutch, crutch, crutch," and all three of them giggled so hard that Mrs. Field called after them, "Stop being so silly and be careful."

"We can't be careful," Marcie said. "We're crutches." And they shrieked with laughter.

Still laughing, Marcie and Kim lowered Poppy onto the wooden floor of the merry-go-round and waited while she turned sideways to straighten her leg.

"Let's go," Kim said. She stood on one side and Marcie on the other, and they started pushing slowly at first and then faster and faster.

"Whee!" Poppy lay on her back and watched the clouds whirl overhead. "I'm getting dizzy."

Marcie and Kim hopped on and they twirled around and around till the merry-go-round slowed down. Then they got off and pushed again until they were going faster than before. They hopped on and rode it until it slowed down. Marcie and Kim pushed and rode and pushed and rode for ten minutes, while Poppy lay on her back, watching the sky. Suddenly they all heard the hoot of a train in the distance. Kim and Marcie jumped off, leaving Poppy on the platform. "We'll be right back," they called, and started running toward the hill.

"Wait," Poppy called. "I'll get my crutches."

"No, stay there," Marcie called back. "We'll come back for you."

Poppy didn't have a choice. She sat up and watched her friends climb up the steep hill. The merry-go-round went slower and slower. It stopped. Poppy put her legs over the side of the merry-go-round. By now Marcie and Kim had disappeared over the top of the hill. Poppy was so mad she felt tears spring to her eyes. How could they just leave her like this? Her mother was sitting on a blanket, not far off, eating a sandwich with one hand and writing in her notebook with the other.

She wasn't going to call for help even if she had to crawl back to the blanket on her hands and knees. She took hold of the top bar of the merry-go-round and pulled herself up. She leaned to her left as far as she could go so her right leg wouldn't drag on the grass. She hopped on her left foot. She hopped again. Then she fell down.

"Poppy!" Her mother came running over. "What are you doing? You're going to break your leg again." She stood there for a second looking angrily down at Poppy, then she ran back for the crutches.

"They just left me here!" Poppy yelled. "They just ran up the hill and forgot about me. Some friends—we bring them on a picnic and feed them and this is what they do. See if I ever, ever ask them on another picnic. See if I ask them anywhere again. Those dopes. Those jerkfaces. I hate them both. They think they're so smart. I had the idea to ask them on the picnic and then they just run off by themselves. I hate them!" she yelled again.

When they got back to the blanket, her mom put her arm around her. "This isn't going to be an easy summer for you, Pumpkin."

"I hate this summer. I hate my cast. I hate everybody." Poppy reached out and yanked a wad of grass from the ground and threw it in the direction Kim and Marcie had gone. She still couldn't see them.

"Look up there," her mother said, pointing overhead. "White sheep."

Poppy sank down on the blanket and looked the other way.

"White sheep, white sheep . . . how does that go?" her mother asked.

"I don't know," Poppy said glumly.

"C'mon, Poppy, let's cheer up."

"No," Poppy said.

Her mother got up on her knees and looked down into Poppy's face. She pulled her ears out and crossed her eyes.

Poppy giggled.

Her mother lay back down on the blanket and put her arm around Poppy. They looked at the white puffs of clouds. "How does it go?" her mother asked.

"White sheep, white sheep," Poppy said.

"On a blue hill,
When the wind stops
You all stand still.
When the wind blows
You walk away slow.
White sheep, white sheep,
Where do you go?"

5

The Big Truth

Poppy was still mad at Marcie and Kim. She had barely spoken to them since the picnic, and when Marcie stopped over to show her a clipping from the *McGregor Beach Weekly*, Poppy didn't even ask her in. Ever since Marcie had been her best friend, Poppy had been the leader. She was the one to come up with the good ideas like putting pine cones in Davey Dickson's boots and dressing up as mermaids for the Neptune Parade. She couldn't forgive Marcie for running off at the picnic. "I'm busy," she said, when Marcie handed her the article. "My dad's coming home tonight and we have to clean up." And she shut the door.

The news article was about her. "Lilac Court Athlete Takes a Tumble," it said. It told how Poppy fell from the top of the maple in her backyard "a distance of twenty feet or so." The article continued, "We'll miss seeing our own little Poppy Field splashing around in the lake this summer and we hope she's back in time for Neptune Carnival. From now on, Poppy, please limit your climbing to stairs and stepping stools." It was signed by Mr. Hoban, the editor of the *Weekly*.

Ordinarily Poppy loved to be in the *McGregor Beach Weekly*, to have the neighbors know that she had won a skiing race or spent Christmas vacation at her grandma's in Maine. But this was terrible. "Aaarrrgh," she groaned.

"What's up?" Tiz said. He had just come in from hauling junk from the garage out to the curb. Their father loved a clean garage as much as he loved a clean house.

"I'm in the *McGregor Beach Weekly*."

"Big deal," Tiz said. "So is every six-year-old who pulls out a tooth."

"It says I fell out of the maple tree." She held up the clipping.

"So?" He looked at the article, pushing up his glasses with his finger just like Mom did.

"I didn't fall out of the tree." She swallowed. "I fell off the roof."

"What?" Tiz put his hands on his hips and stared at her.

She hadn't meant to tell Tiz about the Big Lie but it was like carrying a fifty-pound weight around with her. She had enough problems without having to carry the Big Lie around, too. "Should I tell Mom and Dad?" she asked meekly.

Tiz snorted. "What for? So you can get into more trouble?"

"But they think I was climbing the maple," she argued.

"So what," he said, handing back the clipping. "You broke your leg, either way. Aren't you supposed to be folding your sheets? This living room still looks like a bedroom."

Poppy looked around. Since she had been sleeping downstairs, she had taken over the entire living room. Her clothes were scattered on every chair and tabletop. There were three pairs of baggy shorts that her mother had made for her folded on top of the TV. There were two left shoes in the middle of the room and her beach ball globe still hung from the ceiling.

"Get this stuff picked up," Tiz said, "so I can vacuum." Poppy went around the room picking things up the way the therapist showed her—putting both crutches under one arm and swinging her cast behind her when she bent down. While Tiz vacuumed, she folded her clothes and then her sheets. She put everything in a neat pile and loaded it in Tiz's old canvas paperboy bag. She slipped one of the handles over her head and let the bag fall against her chest. Then she headed for the laundry room.

"Hey, you're pretty handy with that thing," he yelled over the vacuum. "I should have made you carry all that garbage out to the road."

Poppy stuck her tongue out at Tiz, but it

made her feel good to be able to help him clean up. The paperboy bag was his idea. In it she could carry her clothes, her radio, her towel and shampoo, even a sandwich, cookies, and a thermos of lemonade if she wanted to eat in the backyard. She was so sick of being helpless—of not being able to go up and down stairs, of getting stuck in the screen door—that she wanted to scream. Sometimes she did scream.

By the time their mom got back from the grocery store, Tiz and Poppy had the living room sparkling. Tiz even cleaned the windows.

"Do you know what you're going to play?" Mom asked Tiz. Whenever Mr. Field had been away a long time, they always had a special party for his return. Tiz played the piano, and Mrs. Field cooked salmon with capers and cherry pie.

"My Chicken Dance!" Poppy said, looking stricken. "How can I do my Chicken Dance?"

"That's okay, Sweetie. Dad won't expect you to do the Chicken Dance with a broken leg," Mom said.

"But it's a tradition," Poppy said. She knew her father would be crushed if she didn't do her Chicken Dance for his homecoming. When he got home from a long trip he liked everything to be just the same—that's what he always said. He liked routine, just like Poppy. The Chicken Dance had been part of the family routine for three years, ever since Poppy took dance lessons at the Duncan Center. Back then she had a chicken costume and a hat with a yellow beak. Everyone liked her dance so much that she performed it whenever she could, squawking and beating her arms against her sides.

"Why don't you recite that lovely poem about the clouds?" her mother suggested.

"Poop," Poppy said.

Her mother looked stern. "I'm getting tired of that word, Poppy. I don't want to hear you using it again."

"Poo," Poppy said, looking at her mother. She knew she was pushing it.

"You two finish up in the dining room," Mom said. "I've got lots to do in the kitchen before I pick your father up at the airport."

It was after six when her mom and dad pulled up in the driveway.

"Yaaa-aa-ay," Poppy yelled, getting up from the sofa. She crutched over to the door and watched her father get out of the car, his big, bulky body towering over her mother, his wonderful red hair like a sign to everyone on Lilac Court, saying, "Look who's back in town."

"Daddy," she yelled from the doorway.

"Daisy," he yelled back. "Marigold!" It was a joke between them. He always called her a bunch of different flowers before he got the right one.

Tiz ran out and hugged him and then went to get his suitcases.

When her father got to the door, he bent down so she could put her arms around his neck. Then he lifted her up and twirled her around and around. She pressed her face against his scratchy cheek. "Dad, oh, Dad," she said, almost wanting to cry.

"Poppy, my hoppy little Poppy," he thundered, and Poppy remembered how much she had missed his booming voice. His neck was so nice and scratchy and warm and it smelled like Spain. She could go on hugging his neck forever.

When he set her down on the sofa he looked at her cast. "What is this thing?"

Poppy patted her cast, proud that she had something so unusual to show him. "Remember, Dad, I broke my leg?"

"Is that a cast—that long white thing? It looks like a—a sewer pipe. Are you sure there's a leg in there?"

"Sure, I'm sure." Poppy wiggled her toes back and forth. "Look at my toes."

"Well, I want to hear all about this terrible accident of yours but first . . ." He closed his eyes and sniffed. "I smell salmon and capers. Let's eat."

All through dinner Dad told them about Spain, about the mountains, and about a family he had met who had peacocks running around in their yard. The peacocks' names were Cicero and Emmanuella.

"Peacocks are beautiful," said her mother.

"Only Cicero was beautiful," Dad said. "He had a bright blue head and a green tail that spread out behind him like a huge, glittery fan. That tail must have been five feet tall. But poor Emmanuella was drab and brown as a mouse."

Poppy thought it was odd for the man to be decorated in pretty feathers and the woman to be dressed in boring colors. She thought it should be the other way around. "Did you ever go to the Guadalquivir River?" she asked, remembering her globe.

"No," he said, tweaking her nose, "did you ever go to the I Wannascream Stream?"

"Oh, Dad," she said, giggling. It was so nice to have her father home and to be all sitting around the table eating fancy food by candlelight and using the good, pink napkins. Usually, her mother made things that were really plain, like tuna and noodles or hot dogs. If she was really busy, she let them fix their own dinner—usually Wheaties or a peanut butter sandwich.

"I love it when you're home, Dad," she said, putting down her fork and staring at his wide laughing face.

"So do I, Poppy," he said, scooping up the last cherry from his piece of pie. "I miss having a beautiful flower at my table every night."

She smiled, imagining her hair as a bright fringe of red petals around her face.

They all went in the living room, just leaving the dirty dishes on the table because they wanted to keep the party going.

"Are we going to open our presents now?" Poppy asked. Their father always brought them presents when he went away.

"You have to give me your presents first," he said, pulling Poppy onto his lap and nibbling on her ear.

Poppy's heart sank. She thought about the Chicken Dance that she wasn't going to do.

They watched as Tiz sat down at the piano. He didn't give any big introductions when he was going to play. He just took the sheet music out of the bench and started playing "The Maple Leaf Rag." She watched Tiz's fingers bounding up and down the keys, never missing a beat. The whole house seemed to shake. The "Maple Leaf Rag" was so cheerful and full of energy, Poppy really felt like getting up and dancing. She felt new steps and twirls spring up in her mind. It would be even better than the Chicken Dance. If only she didn't have the stupid cast on.

When Tiz finished, they all clapped and cheered. Tiz just sat there with his hands folded. He didn't get up and take a bow or wave his arms over his head the way Poppy would have. But he looked pretty happy when their dad went over and started thumping him on the back. "That was fantastic, Tiz. I'm so proud that you stuck with it all these years."

Now Poppy felt terrible. Once she had taken piano lessons and quit after only three months. She hated, absolutely hated, practicing. Practice time always came when her friends were roller skating by her window or playing lawn tag across the street. It was awful sitting still for that long, thinking about her fingers. Playing piano was easy for Tiz, though—he liked to sit still. That was what he did best.

Now her father looked at her and pulled his lips down in a frown. "I guess I'm not going to see your Chicken Dance, am I?"

She shook her head.

"But I'll bet you have something even better planned, don't you?" He leaned close to Poppy's face as if she had a secret to tell him.

Poppy shook her head. "I can't do anything."

"Well," he said, "that doesn't sound like the Poppy I left behind, my Poppy Field who was always blooming with exciting things to do. I guess having a broken leg just cramps your style, doesn't it?"

Poppy didn't know she was going to feel so bad. Her father was disappointed in her and she was disappointed in herself. Maybe she should have recited one of the dumb poems she had memorized. Now it was too late. He was handing a present to Tiz.

"It's from Madrid, Tiz. I bought it from a retired army officer."

Tiz tore off the gold foil and underneath was

a long, metal sword in a metal holder with tassels hanging off. Tiz held it up and looked at the point.

"Careful," Mom said. "Don't cut yourself."

He bought Poppy's mom some silver bracelets and also a long black cape with a red lining. She tried it on and it swirled around her ankles. "I look like Mata Hari," she said, lifting the edge of the cape under her eyes, like she was a spy.

The mention of Mata Hari made Poppy think of the Big Lie. She looked away from her mother and down at the floor.

"This is for you," her father said, handing Poppy a package in shiny foil. "I think you'll really like this."

When Poppy tore off the wrapping and opened the box she saw something gold inside. She lifted it out and held it up. It was slim, shiny gold pants, rounded at the bottoms.

"Toreador pants," her mother said. "All that gold braid down the sides—why, they're lovely."

"That's what the bullfighters wear," he told Poppy, "when they go in the ring. I hope they fit."

Poppy's mother gave her a quick look that said, "Please be nice," but Poppy didn't care. She was crushed. "Of course they don't fit," she said, throwing them down. "Nothing fits except baggy old shorts and baggy underwear. I hate those stupid pants. You might as well take them back to Spain and get your money back. I wait and wait and wait for you to come home and then you bring me old tor—torso pants."

"Oh, Lord," her father said, putting his arm around her. "What a lunkhead I am. I forgot about your cast. All I could think about was my whirling dervish whirling around in toreador pants. I should have my ears chopped off. I'm going to take you out tomorrow and buy you something that does fit—a pink party dress, how's that?"

Poppy was feeling so terrible that she wanted her father to keep feeling terrible, too. "I don't want a pink party dress," she sniffed.

"Geeze, Poppy," Tiz said. "Way to be a spoiled brat."

"I am not," Poppy yelled. "Leave me alone. Nobody understands what it's like to have a broken leg. Nobody cares. I thought Dad would understand, but he doesn't. He's just like everyone else."

"Well, why don't you tell me," he said, taking her hands in his. "Tell me exactly how it happened."

Poppy's heart sank. "I can't talk about it," she said.

"It's very simple," her mother said. "She was climbing the maple tree."

"Climbing the maple!" her father roared. "What was she doing in that huge tree?"

"She's been climbing it since she was five," her mother said calmly.

"Never," he yelled, thumping the arm of the sofa. "You should never have allowed it. I would never have allowed a ten-year-old girl to climb a fifty-foot tree."

"Oh, come on, Sam. You're out of touch. Poppy can climb that tree better than Tiz can. Better than you, too, I'll bet. When was the last time you watched her climb a tree?"

"Never!" her father roared. "I never watched her and I never want to watch her. And if she hadn't done it, she wouldn't be hobbling around here like a three-legged pup!"

"Don't yell at me, Sam Field!"

"Well, I guess I can yell in my own house!"

Poppy looked from her mother to her father. He had only been back from Spain for a few hours and they were fighting. Over her. "Stop!" She hopped up on her good leg and held out her hands. "I didn't climb the maple tree. I climbed out on the roof. I didn't fall out of the tree. I fell off the roof."

"What!" her father roared.

"What!" her mother screamed.

"Dummy," Tiz said.

6

Cootie

Poppy was lying outside on the chaise lounge with the blue cloth over her face, feeling sorry for herself. Marcie had called to apologize for running off and leaving Poppy on the merry-go-round and she asked if Poppy wanted to go to the Sugar Bowl for a sundae. But Poppy was grounded. It was stupid to be grounded for something she had done twenty-one days ago, but her mom and dad said they wanted to impress on her never to climb on the roof again.

Even though it was a relief not to have to carry the Big Lie around with her anymore, Poppy felt that her parents should have been more understanding. A person with a broken leg should never be grounded. It was just too, too depressing.

As she lay there thinking about it, she realized it wasn't her parents' fault that she was grounded—it was Cootie's fault. It was all a part of the terrible curse Cootie had put on her. Poppy wished with all her heart that Cootie didn't live next door, that she lived in Spain or Scotland or somewhere far away. As she lay thinking about Cootie, she smelled smoke coming from next door. Cootie was burning her trash again. Poppy took off the cloth and sat up, sniffing hard to see if she could detect the odor of boiling cats. It smelled like hot vinegar. Maybe that was what she boiled them in, Poppy thought, to disguise the smell. She was about to lay back down when she saw something she had never noticed before. There was a gap in the hedge just beyond her lounge chair and there was also a gap in the blankets on Cootie's line. Through it she could see the leg of Cootie's black pants.

Poppy leaned way over trying to see the rest of Cootie, but the hedge blocked her view. She wondered what Cootie did in her backyard. Did she weed the flower beds like her mother did? She knew Cootie didn't cut her lawn. That was what some of the neighbors complained about. That and her raggedy flag. Maybe Cootie lay outside in the sun and read books like her mother. But Cootie didn't seem anything like her mother. What did she do in that big house all by herself?

Poppy leaned down and picked up her crutches from the grass. She certainly wasn't going to read the boring poetry book her mother had sent outside with her or start drawing in the sketchbook from Marcie. The two books were still inside the paperboy bag that she had brought outside along with her lunch. Hoisting herself up from the lounge chair, she paused to position her crutches under her arms.

Even on the grass, full of dips and bumps, Poppy was a skilled crutcher. She could make her way in and out of the house without getting caught in the screen door, and up and down the porch step. Her hands had started to become tough and callused from pressing down on the hand bar of her crutches. She wished there was some kind of crutch race for Neptune Carnival. She knew she could win.

Poppy crutched over to her mother's flower bed and admired the poppies. There were dozens of them in bloom now, bright red clumps of them, and here and there, single poppies of softest pink. Poppy watched as an orange butterfly landed on a poppy and then lifted and alighted on another. Pretty soon it fluttered up in the air and then down and then up again, as if it weren't sure where it was going. Poppy wished she could turn into a butterfly. She would know right where to go. She would fly straight for the Sugar Bowl and order a Triple Threat Banana Split. What a shock it would be for Marcie and her mom to see Poppy come fluttering in through the door.

She snorted just thinking about it. Then, cautiously, she started moving toward the hole in the hedge, slowly, slowly, as if Cootie could see her right through the hedge. When she got to the gap, she stopped with her back to the hedge, the way police officers always did when they were about to enter a dangerous house. She balanced herself on one crutch and looked over her shoulder through the gap. Cootie was still there, standing in front of an old brick barbecue pit, watching the flames.

Since Cootie's back was to her, Poppy turned around and faced the gap in the hedge. She watched as Cootie dumped another bag of trash into the fire and stirred it with a black poker. It looked like papers and rotten fruit, not cats, coming out of the bag. It was the first time Poppy had really looked at Cootie's whole self. She had short gray hair and a big yellow bow tied around her neck. Poppy was surprised that Cootie was so little. The bottoms of her black pants dragged on the ground. Poppy wondered which leg was the wooden one. Did she have a shoe on the leg or was it just a wooden stick at the bottom? Greg Piper told her that an alligator bit off Cootie's leg, but her mother said that she tipped over on a tractor when she was a young woman, and it crushed her leg.

Poppy noticed that on the ledge of the barbecue pit was a big, turquoise, stuffed poodle. It had a pink bow tied under its neck, like Cootie's yellow bow. Everyone knew that Cootie liked stuffed animals, because there were dozens of them piled up in the back window of her car—so many that she probably couldn't see out.

As Poppy watched, she could hear Cootie talking in her raspy little voice. But who was she talking to? Maybe she was chanting the words to another curse that she was going to put on someone. Poppy shuddered. Just then Cootie put the poker down and turned to the blue poodle. "I think that's such a zesty smell, don't you?" she said, picking up the dog. "It's a spicy, nicey smell. Better than flowers, isn't it? Better than popcorn. A spicy, nicey fire warms the heart, doesn't it, Stanley? Don't you agree, Stanley?" she repeated, patting the dog's nose.

Poppy's mouth dropped open. She was talking to the poodle. Cootie was crazy. She talked to stuffed animals. Now Poppy was really scared. What if Cootie turned around and caught her spying again? She moved back from the hedge and hobbled quickly back to the chair. "Oh, my gosh," she said out loud. "Cootie's a crazy old witch." She was too jumpy to lay back down with the cloth over her face. She felt like running around the yard or jumping on her bicycle and racing around the block three times. She leaned over and took the sketchbook out of the bag. She tore out the first page and folded it in half, lengthwise, and then folded it again and again. She tapped the nose of the paper airplane against the wrought iron arm and then pointed it to the sky. "Whoosh."

It took off sailing and landed halfway across

the yard under the pussy willow. She ripped another sheet out and made another one, sleeker than the first. She sailed it in the other direction and it landed in her mother's flower garden, nose down in the poppies. She made another and another until the yard was littered with white paper airplanes. She ripped the final piece of paper from the tablet and folded and creased her last airplane. She was going to send this one all the way over to the Sugar Bowl. She picked up a pencil and wrote on the wing, "Greetings from your pal Poppy." Then she pointed it nose up into the sun and pushed it off. The white paper plane caught on an up-draft and rose skyward across the yard. To her surprise, it sailed over the hedge and disap-peared into Cootie's yard.

"Ooops," Poppy said, wincing. She decided the best thing she could do was grab her crutches and hurry back in the house just in case Cootie was still back there. As she bent for her crutches, her father came out of the house.

"Poppy, I'm going to give you five minutes to clean up these paper airplanes before I cut the lawn. Five minutes and I don't want any excuses about your leg. You made the mess. You can clean it up."

"But I have to go in the house for a minute," Poppy said feebly.

"Now," he barked, and he went back in the house.

"What a grouch," she grumbled, getting out of the lounge chair. When her father was away she only remembered the best things about him, like how he sang "Ats Amoray" in the shower and cooked pancakes on Sunday mornings. She forgot how fussy he was about having everything cleaned up. He hollered if somebody forgot to screw the cap back on the toothpaste.

It wasn't easy picking up the airplanes from the lawn. The grass was a lot more uneven than the floor. She had to lean way over and keep her balance on her good leg. When she got an airplane she stuffed it in her canvas bag, which was around her neck.

"Thirty-six," she said, picking one up from under the flowering almond. She had picked up thirty-six paper airplanes and she hadn't lost her balance once. She bet no one else on crutches could balance as well as she could. If there was ever a balancing-on-crutches contest, she would win it, she knew she would.

Poppy was getting hot and sweaty. Her leg inside her cast was itching like mad. How could that crazy Cootie enjoy a fire on a hot day like this? She would give a million dollars to be able to go down and jump in the lake. She spotted one last airplane over by the hedge. Poppy crutched over and leaned way down. "Got it," she said as she straightened up. When she stood up, she came face-to-face with Cootie.

Cootie was holding out the paper airplane that had sailed into her yard. Her face above the yellow bow was pleated into a hundred and fifty wrinkles and her eyes stared out at Poppy like little blue marbles. She threw the airplane at Poppy's feet, and without a word, she disappeared back into the hedge.

7

Bobadil

Poppy was eating Wheaties and practicing a poem in her head. Tiz was playing the invisible piano. That's what she called it when Tiz moved his fingers up and down the table like he was practicing.

She picked up her cereal bowl and drank noisily.

"Geeze," Tiz said, looking up. "Eat the bowl, too, why don't you?"

Poppy ignored him. "I'm ready, Mom."

Her mother stopped typing and rolled her chair over to where Poppy sat. "I'm all ears."

Another of her mother's weird expressions, Poppy thought, picturing dozens of ears sticking out of her mother's face and arms and legs. She took a deep breath. "Bobadil," she said, "by James Reeves."

"Far from far
Lives Bobadil
In a tall house
On a tall hill.

Out from the high
Top window-sill
On a clear night
Leans Bobadil.

To touch the moon,
To catch a star,
To keep in her tall house
Far from far."

"Well," her mother said, patting Poppy's

cheek, "what a nice little poem." She handed Poppy her dollar. "I like Bobadil."

"You do?" Poppy was surprised. Bobadil seemed like a witch to her.

"Oh, yes. Wouldn't you like to catch a star and put it in a special little box somewhere? Or hang it on a string and wear it around your neck?"

"But she's creepy." Poppy made a face. "Thumping around in that big, old, dark house, all alone. Far from far," Poppy echoed, and she thought of Cootie. She seemed to live "far from far," even though she lived right next door. She suddenly realized that she had chosen 'Bobadil' because it reminded her of Cootie. "Don't you think she's creepy?" she said again.

"No," her mother insisted. "I think 'Bobadil' is strong and mysterious. That's what makes poetry fun. It can make you feel one way and me feel another way. A poem that makes you feel sad might make me feel silly."

"Like 'The Jabberwocky,'" Tiz said. That was the thing about Tiz. He was so quiet you would forget he was there, and then he would butt in all of a sudden.

"Yeah," Poppy agreed. "I just don't know why the Jabberwock had to have his head chopped off." Back when Tiz used to recite poems, too, before he got a real job, he recited "The Jabberwocky," and Poppy liked the whiffling, burbling monster with eyes of flame. After hearing the poem, she started whiffling and burbling whenever she got the chance. "Whiffle, whiffle, whiffle, burble, burble, burble," she said for old time's sake.

"If you two are done with your breakfast, would you clear out of here?" Mom said. "I have to make a casserole, and Dad has a bunch of paperwork he wants to spread out on the table."

Poppy followed Tiz into the living room. She sat on her bed with her legs stretched out. It was really the sofa, but after four weeks of sleeping on it she thought of it as her bed. "What are you going to do?" she asked Tiz.

He sat down at the piano. "Practice."

Poppy sighed. Her entire family was busy doing separate things. They should be rallying around her, making sure she wasn't bored. What had her father come all the way from Spain for if he wasn't going to pay the slightest bit of attention to her? "I want to go swimming," she said. She picked up a Magic Marker from the coffee table and wrote "I want to go swimming" across the top of her cast. There was hardly any room left anywhere else. Everyone who came over had signed the cast with the marker. Her fourth grade teacher, Mrs. Robb, had even stopped by to see how she was doing and she wrote "I hope you're walking soon—and running and jumping and dancing and swimming." She went around Poppy's leg two times.

Poppy said louder, "I want to go swimming!"

"Shut up, Poppy," Tiz said. He was playing something that sounded like waterfalls.

"But I want to go swimming," she whined.

"So go swimming," Tiz said. He turned around. "Just close your eyes and imagine yourself down at the beach. Feel the water rippling over your hot skin. You're stroking with one arm, then the other, kicking with your legs. One anna two anna one anna two. Just feel it."

Poppy closed her eyes and did as Tiz instructed. She imagined the cool water rushing over her as she slid through the water toward the raft. She felt the rhythm of her breathing. "Hey," she said, "it works."

"Sure," he said. "Visualization. You can still practice swimming while your leg is in a cast." He started playing again.

"One anna two anna one anna two," she counted in her head. She rode the cool, buoyant water out past the diving platform, all the way to the red and white markers and back. She saw the water cascading off her arm as she lifted it in the sun, felt the roll of her head as she breathed. The cast was gone and she felt like a quick, silver fish gliding through the water.

Poppy lay stretched out on the sofa swimming around and around McGregor Lake. She swam for at least ten minutes. Then she had a thought. She could practice visualizing for

Neptune Carnival right down at the beach. She hadn't yet walked down to the beach on her crutches, but it was only two blocks.

"Tiz," she said, pulling herself up. "I'm going to the beach."

"Uhh," he said, without turning around. When he was playing piano he was in his own world, like Mom at her typewriter.

Poppy pushed open the screen door with her crutch and stepped out onto the porch. It was a brilliant July day and it looked like everyone on her street was outside enjoying it. Mr. Williams was out washing his car. Mr. and Mrs. Burke were walking down the sidewalk with their twin boys, Ike and Mike, probably walking over to Winterberry Street to visit Grandma. Her old babysitter, Lori, was lying on a blanket in a red bikini, getting a suntan. Poppy waved at Lori without stopping. She was trying to catch up with the Burkes. She wanted to see if she could crutch faster than they could walk. Plant and swing, plant and swing. She watched her shadow lean and straighten in the sun. She was moving at racing speed when she got to Cootie's front sidewalk and something made her stop. The yard, unlike the Burkes' yard and all the other yards full of flowers and tidy lawns, was dark and hidden. Two willows hung their tangled branches over the sidewalk and raggedy shrubs blocked out almost the entire view of her yard.

She took a few steps onto the lawn and looked up at Cootie's bedroom window. Bobadil, she thought, and she pictured Cootie leaning out and snatching a star out of the sky. "In her tall house, far from far," she whispered. The big brown house looked as if nobody lived in it. The dark shutters hung crookedly and there were deep cobwebs above the front door. At this very moment, Cootie could be looking down on her from some hidden place, uttering more curses. Poppy shuddered and turned back to the sidewalk. She started to move in the direction of the beach, but she spotted Cootie's mailbox next to the gravel driveway. She thought about Bobadil and how much her mother liked her. In her shorts pocket was a copy of "Bobadil." Quickly, before she could change her mind, Poppy pulled out the poem and stuffed it in Cootie's rusty old mailbox. Then, before Cootie could come chasing after her, Poppy hurried away down the sidewalk. Plant and swing, plant and swing.

Her breath was coming very fast and she could feel her cheeks burning. What a stupid thing to do. What would Cootie do when she found the poem in her mailbox? Maybe she would make Poppy break her other leg.

She crutched down the dusty road to the lake, careful to avoid the potholes. She had never walked to the beach before. And she had never gone alone. She always rode her bike with two or three of her friends, laughing and peddling pell-mell to see who could be first in the water. Now she looked around at the big trees lining the roadside. They had leaves like bright green hearts and tiny white flowers. Did all trees have flowers, she wondered, sniffing the honey fragrance they spilled into the air. She wondered why she had never noticed those trees before. Maybe because she was always going so fast when she came down this road.

It was a hot day and Poppy's T-shirt was sticking to her back. Her armpits hurt from the crutches and her hands were sore from pressing on the hand rests. She stopped at the side of the road to catch her breath and she noticed a clump of yellow flowers at her feet, like dozens of dangling little bells. She stepped back onto the road so she wouldn't crush them. Just around the bend was the beach. She could hear the squeals of kids and the sproing, sproing of the diving board and then the lifeguard booming into the megaphone: "No pushing on the raft."

She planted her crutches and started moving forward. Suddenly, around the bend came a little blond girl dragging a beach towel. She was looking down the road and crying as if her heart was broken.

Poppy stopped. "What's wrong, honey?" But the little girl stomped her foot and cried louder.

"Where's your mother?" Poppy asked.

"Mommy!" the little girl wailed. She sat down in the middle of the road and curled herself into an unhappy little ball.

Poppy wanted to put her arms around the little girl, but she was afraid it would upset her.

"Jennifer!" Around the bend came a woman in sunglasses, her hair flying. "Jennifer, I've been going nuts. Where have you been?"

"Mommy!" The little girl jumped up and flung herself in her mother's arms. They both laughed and hugged each other and went on down the road without even noticing Poppy.

Poppy went on, relieved that they had found each other. It was a scary thing to feel lost and alone, even for a minute. As soon as she came in view of the lake, Greg Piper spotted her. "Hey, Poppy," he yelled. He came splashing out of the water. "Hey! Did you walk all the way down here on your crutches?"

"Sure," she said. "No big deal." But her leg hurt and she was more tired than she would admit to Greg. She looked longingly at the benches along the breakwall. "I just came down to see what you guys were doing."

"Playing water volleyball. We're creaming Matt and Jim and Marcie," he said, grinning. Poppy and Greg usually played on the same side and she felt a twinge of envy. "Hey," Greg said, "wanna play?"

"Oh, sure," she said, rolling her eyes. "Just jump in the lake with my cast. Right."

"Sissy," he said, flicking water at her, and he ran back across the beach and dove off the breakwall into the lake.

"Greg Piper," the lifeguard blared into her megaphone, "no diving off the breakwall."

But Greg didn't even look back. Poppy watched his wet brown head surface right beside the volleyball net, and in a minute he and five friends were popping the ball into the air, diving sideways and falling down, splashing water on everyone within twelve feet. Poppy watched, remembering how much fun they all had last summer, playing water volleyball.

She decided to head for the beach on the breakwall, but when she planted her crutches in the sandy beach, it was a strange sensation. They slid all over the place. She decided she'd better take tiny steps or she would fall down. It was a difficult journey across the beach. Instead of lifting herself over the sand, she sunk down into it. The bottom of her cast was getting all sandy and so were her toes. She hoped sand wasn't going up her cast, but she was afraid it was. She could almost feel it picking and itching all the way up her leg.

When she finally made it to the breakwall, the lifeguard, whose name was Tina, looked down from her stand. "Poppy, I can't believe you did that," she said admiringly.

"It was easy," Poppy lied. She was panting from the effort and her face was all red and sweaty. What she wanted to do most of all was sink down on the beach and rest. But she didn't want Tina to think she was a sissy, too. She crutched out a little farther to the edge of the breakwall. "Hey, Greg," she yelled. "Hey Marcie, hey Kim." She waved at her friends. When she lifted her arm, her crutch went over into the water. And one second later, so did Poppy, down into the cool blue water of McGregor Lake.

It was Tina who pulled her out of the water. But within two minutes everyone at the beach came running over to see Poppy stretched out on the breakwall with her big white, wet cast.

"Somebody send for her mother," Tina said, covering Poppy with a blanket, even though it was about a hundred degrees out.

"What happened?" somebody asked.

"She jumped in," somebody else said.

"No," another voice said, "Greg Piper pushed her."

"I did not, you jerk," Greg announced. He shoved through the crowd and kneeled down beside her, his red, freckled face quite serious. "Hey, Poppy, you want me and Matt to carry you home? We can make a chair with our arms. It'd be a cinch."

Poppy just looked sorrowfully at her wet cast. She knew she was in trouble. "Don't get it wet," Dr. Rosenberg had cautioned.

If people would stop making such a fuss about it, maybe she could stretch out in the sun until it dried. And she wouldn't have to tell her mom and dad. She wondered how she could get all these people to keep her secret.

"You're in trouble, Poppy," a voice said. "Big trouble." It was Tiz. He came through the crowd of people and knelt beside Poppy. "Mom sent me down here to bring you back. Too bad I didn't get here a little earlier."

Poppy still didn't say anything. She just pinched her lips together so she wouldn't cry. Tiz picked her up and headed for his yellow car and Tina followed with her crutches.

"Bye, Poppy," Tina said, putting the crutches in the backseat. "I hope you feel better. Bye, Tiz." She added, "Why don't you ever come down to the beach and see me?"

"Oh," he said, looking surprised. "Oh, I will." He waved at Tina and pulled out. Then he stopped the car and yelled after Tina's bright orange bikini, "Thanks for rescuing Poppy."

"She didn't rescue me!" Poppy yelled. "I could have climbed back on the breakwall myself."

"You're in trouble," Tiz said. "Big trouble."

8

One Pink Cast

Poppy's mother took her pencil out of her hair and pointed it at her. "Poppy, I swear, sometimes you act like a two-year-old," she said. "Do I have to watch you every second?"

Her father got red in the face. "You're grounded!" he yelled. "You're grounded for the rest of the summer. Don't even think of leaving this backyard. I'm going to hire a big watchdog to sit beside you and keep an eye on you."

"Now, Sam . . . " her mother cautioned.

"Don't 'Now, Sam' me," her father snorted. "Poppy has a broken leg and she still thinks she can act like Superwoman. People with broken legs don't go marching around the neighborhood on crutches. They don't hobble out to the beach, and they certainly don't perch on the breakwall where they're liable to fall in." He glared at Poppy. "Now I suppose you think you can just lie in the sun until this thing dries out."

Even though Poppy did think that might work, she didn't say anything. She hated it when her father yelled at her. She wanted her father to pick her up and to call her his special star.

"No," he huffed, "now we have to drive you to the doctor and have a new cast put on. Maybe that's what you want to do on a Saturday afternoon, but I've got work to do."

As it turned out, Poppy's mother drove her to see Dr. Rosenberg. "Is he going to yell at me, too?" Poppy asked nervously.

"He won't be pleased," her mother replied, turning into the parking lot of the gray brick clinic. "But I doubt if he will yell." She patted Poppy's hand.

Dr. Rosenberg sat Poppy on a high bed covered with white paper, just as he had done on all her other visits. He touched the cast with both hands and felt inside it at the top and bottom. Then he stood back and looked at Poppy. "Would you like to tell me how this happened?"

Poppy swallowed and looked into his dark little eyes. She was still worried about the yelling. "I fell in the lake."

"Ah," he said, "you wanted to go swimming?"

"No," she said. "I mean yes, but I didn't mean to. It was an accident."

"You know what we usually do when people get their casts wet?"

Poppy bit her thumbnail. "Yell at them?"

Dr. Rosenberg laughed. "No," he said, and patted her soggy cast. "No, I don't ever want to lose my patience with my patients."

He and Poppy's mother laughed at this joke, but Poppy was too worried. What if she had to stay in the cast an extra two weeks?

"Sometimes people get their cast just a little wet. When that happens we just whip out a trusty hair dryer and blow it dry again," Dr. Rosenberg said.

Poppy's heart lifted like a helium balloon. "You mean I don't have to have a new cast put on?"

He shook his head. "I'm afraid you weren't so lucky, Poppy. This cast is really soaked, and I feel sand inside. When you fell in the lake, you must have scooped up sand. I'll bet it feels itchy on your poor old leg, doesn't it?"

She nodded. It felt like an army of little red ants.

"Okay," he said. "We're going to have you out of this wet thing in just a few minutes. We'll scrub off your leg, take an X ray, and fix you up with a nice, clean cast. Just think, you can start collecting autographs all over again."

Dr. Rosenberg took out a small, white saw and turned it on. It made a high, whizzing sound like tomatoes in the blender. "You'll feel heat when I'm cutting, but it won't hurt you," he promised.

He started at the top of her leg and cut slowly and carefully down to the bottom of her foot. Little bursts of white powder came from her cast as he cut, but she didn't feel anything but the jiggle of the saw and a little warm feeling traveling down her leg with the saw. Pretty soon he cut the other side and lifted the cast off her leg. Poppy stared down at her bare leg. Then she reached and touched it. It felt weird to be able to touch her skin again. She knew it was her leg, but it didn't feel like her leg. And it didn't look like her leg. "Why is it so white?" she asked Dr. Rosenberg.

"Because it hasn't seen the sunshine for four weeks," he said. He took a small, wet towel and cleaned all the sand off her leg. After the X rays, he sat her back on the paper-covered bed. "I think white is kind of a boring color, don't you? How about a blue cast or a green one?"

"Really?" Poppy wasn't sure if he was joking. "Can I have any color? Can I have pink?"

"One pink cast coming up." He wrapped her leg in layers of gooey pink gauze, starting at the bottom of her foot and going all the way up again. When it dried, her cast was a bright pink, the color of bubble gum. "Beautiful," he said, helping her down from the bed.

"How soon till I get it off for good?" she asked, positioning her crutches under her arm.

"Umm," he said, rubbing his ear. "Hard to say. It looks pretty good. Maybe four weeks, maybe less."

"By August fifth?" she asked, crossing both her fingers.

"Doctors don't make promises," he said. "But patients do." He tapped the end of her nose. "Promise me you'll stay out of the lake."

When they got back in the car, her mom turned the car in the opposite direction of their house.

"Where are we going?" Poppy asked, from the backseat.

"Oh, I just feel like a banana split," her mother said, smiling at Poppy in the rearview mirror. "How about you?"

"Oh, Mom." Poppy heaved a sigh of relief. "Aren't you mad at me anymore?"

"No, Sweetie. I know it was an accident. I know you feel as badly as we do about falling in the lake."

"Worse!" Poppy said. "Honest, I feel worse. Tell Dad not to buy a guard dog, Mom. I won't go down to the beach anymore, I promise. I don't want Dad to be mad at me."

Her mother put her blinker on at the Sugar Bowl. "Oh, Pop, you know Daddy. He gets as furious as a tornado, but in three minutes it all blows over. He just can't stand to think of you hurting yourself again."

Poppy's mother parked the car and came around to help Poppy out. She hurried ahead of Poppy and pulled open the big glass door so Poppy could walk through. She hadn't been to the Sugar Bowl since the last day of school, when her mom had taken her and Kim and Marcie to celebrate passing into the fifth grade. Everything looked strange. She looked around at the red checkered curtains and the white, glass-topped tables and tried to remember if they were new. She had never noticed them before. She didn't even recognize the girl who worked behind the counter.

While they waited for their banana splits, Poppy thought how everything at the Sugar Bowl was different. It even smelled different. Very quietly, so no one would notice, she turned her head from side to side and sniffed. Melted caramels. She never remembered it smelling like anything before. She sniffed again. Now it smelled like strawberries. And that picture of Elvis Presley—had it always been over the cash register?

She started to think how everything in her life had changed since she broke her leg. The grass and flowers and the trees looked different. She had stopped doing all the things she used to do, like roller skate and swim. She couldn't even remember her Chicken Dance anymore. And she hardly ever saw Marcie or Kim or any of her friends. She just sat around in the backyard and read poems or listened to the radio. Sometimes she peeked through the hedge at Cootie. Cootie, she thought. Cootie was the one who had made her different. She didn't see the same or smell the same. Her friends were gone. She didn't do anything the same anymore. Cootie's curse had turned her into a different person.

"Yumm," her mom said. "Isn't this delicious?"

Poppy hadn't even noticed the banana split in front of her. She picked up her spoon. Then she put it down. "Mom," she said, "it wasn't my fault I fell in the lake. It was Cootie's."

Her mom started to smile, but then she changed her mind when she looked at Poppy. She licked whipped cream off her lip. "What do you mean?"

Poppy took a deep breath. This was harder than the Big Lie. But she couldn't keep it inside her any longer. "Cootie put a curse on me for spying on her. I'm not your daughter anymore. I'm someone else. I'm unlucky and I'm clumsy and I don't have friends and I—I—" To her horror, tears started to fill her eyes. She looked around to see if anyone noticed. "I'm weird, Mom," she sniffed.

"Oh, Poppy." Her mom got up and started to come around the table, and Poppy knew she was going to hug her.

"Don't," she hissed. Being hugged by her mother in the Sugar Bowl would be worse than crying in the Sugar Bowl.

Her mother sat back down. "Sweetheart," she whispered, leaning way over so her face was close to Poppy's, "I don't know why you think Cootie put a curse on you. But I promise you it isn't true."

"It is true," Poppy insisted. "You don't understand. I'm not the same."

Her mother looked thoughtful. She poked her glasses. "No, you're not the same," she agreed. "When you had chicken pox, you didn't feel the same, did you?"

"No, but—"

Her mother held up her hand. "When you have the flu, you don't feel the same, do you?"

"No, but—"

"If you can't run and you can't swim and you can't ride your bike, you're not going to act the same. And maybe you're just a teensy bit crabbier than usual. Maybe you scared some of your friends away, did you ever think of that?"

Poppy shrugged. "But why does everything look different? Why does it smell different?"

"I think when you're alone, you notice things you don't notice when you're with your friends. When you're walking instead of running, you might even smell things you never smelled before."

Poppy thought of the heart-shaped leaves she had noticed on the tree by the beach road and the honey-smelling flowers. "But Cootie made me break my leg. She made me fall in the lake. She hates me!"

"She didn't make you do those things—you

did them yourself, Sweetie. Mrs. Kootabelli is just a poor, lonely old lady."

"But, Mom, she's crazy," Poppy said, leaning forward. "She talks to this big stuffed animal."

Her mother patted her hand. "Who would you talk to if you lived all alone?"

"I'm never going to live alone," Poppy insisted. "I'm always going to live with you and Dad and Tiz."

"Well isn't that nice? We can all grow old together." Her mother started eating her banana split again. "Maybe you could get your curse lifted if you made friends with Mrs. Kootabelli."

Poppy shook her head. "She really is weird, Mom. Honest, I know she doesn't like me."

"Why not take her some flowers or—I know." Her mother's face brightened and her eyes grew wide behind her glasses. "You can write her a poem."

Poppy sighed. "What a dumb idea. She doesn't even like poems. Today, I put 'Bobadil' in her mailbox. I'll bet she didn't like it one bit."

"Why Poppy . . ." Her mother's face got all soft and lovey. "What a sweet thing to do. You're my kind, bright, thoughtful Poppy Field." Her mother squeezed her hand.

Poppy picked up her spoon and started eating her banana split—it was starting to go soupy. She loved it when her mom said how kind and thoughtful she was. "I don't know," she said, chewing on a cherry. "What would I say?"

"Tell her what a good heart she has," her mother suggested.

"Like how?" Poppy said, getting into the melted caramel.

"Let's see." Her mother put down her spoon and closed her eyes.

Poppy couldn't believe it. Was she really going to write a poem to Cootie?

9

Poet

Poppy threw her pencil in the air. "I'm ready," she called. "Hurry."

When her mother came into the living room, Poppy stood up. "Poem for Mrs. Kootabelli," she said, "by Poppy Field." She and her mother exchanged smiles.

> *"The little lady in the big, brown house,*
> *Crept around as quiet as a mouse.*
> *If she got lonely when the day would end,*

She sat and talked to her animal friend.
She liked to watch the setting sun,
She always walked, she'd never run."

Her mother clapped and cheered. "What a wonderful poem, Poppy. It's a perfect poem for Mrs. Kootabelli."

"Will she like it?" Poppy asked.

"She'll be honored," her mother said, "to think you wrote a poem especially for her. Sam and Tiz," she called upstairs, "come down and hear Poppy's poem."

Poppy read her poem again. She read slowly and carefully so they would be able to tell that everything rhymed. When she was done she dropped her crutches on the floor and bowed from the waist. Tiz and her mom and dad cheered and clapped.

"My daughter, the poet," her dad said, picking her up and hugging her. "And we thought all you could do was run and jump and swim and whirl around."

When he lowered her to the floor, Poppy

said, "I know, Dad. I never wrote a poem before." She felt happier than she had felt since she broke her leg. Her mom and dad were proud of her again and she was proud of herself. Writing a poem was different than winning at swimming. It was not loud with water splashing and people yelling and arms and legs kicking. It was like something kicking inside her, like a lot of energy inside her heart. She had pictured Cootie creeping around like a little mouse and she really thought about how Cootie felt when she talked to her blue poodle— lonely, just like her mother said. Poetry made you go out of yourself and imagine what it was like to be somebody else. Poppy was so excited she said, "I'm going to write another poem."

"Bravo," her dad said. "That's what they say to the bullfighter when he scores a victory."

"Encore," her mom said. "That's what you say when you want somebody to do something again."

"Neat," Tiz said. "That's what you say when something is neat."

Before her mom went back in the kitchen, she handed Poppy a dollar. "That's for memorizing a poem."

"My own poem," Poppy said gleefully. "I'm going to be rich."

For the rest of the afternoon, Poppy sat out in the sunshine and worked on another poem for Cootie. She wanted it to have mystery and power like "Bobadil," but she wanted Cootie to know it was about her, so her first line was: "Mrs. Kootabelli lived all alone." What could she say about Mrs. Kootabelli that was friendly, that would tell her she had a good heart like her mother said? Maybe she should just say, "She had a good heart." She wrote:

Mrs. Kootabelli lived all alone.
She had a good heart.

Now what rhymed with alone and what rhymed with heart? Alone, grown, phone, tone, bone, stone, she thought. She wrote: "She gave her dog a bone." Now she had to find a rhyme for heart. Part, smart, dart, cart, start. She thought about saying something nice about Cootie again. "She wasn't dumb, she was smart," she wrote. Now she looked at her whole poem:

Mrs. Kootabelli lived all alone.
She had a good heart.
She gave her dog a bone.
She wasn't dumb, she was smart.

Poppy frowned. Everything rhymed, but she wasn't sure this poem was as good as her first one. Maybe she shouldn't use that third line about the dog. After all, Cootie didn't have a real dog who ate bones. And it was silly to talk about giving her stuffed dog a bone. She wanted this to be a good poem like "Bobadil." She decided to think about it for a while, so she lay back in the lounge chair and put the blue cloth over her face.

When she was under the blue cloth it was as if she was all alone, like she was "far from far."

She felt the silver stars pressing into her face and she thought about the stars Bobadil pulled from the sky. Maybe Cootie sat up in her bedroom window and watched the stars and the moon. Moon, she thought, almost rhymed with alone. Her mother had told her that it didn't matter if everything rhymed in a poem. What mattered was the feeling. She liked the feeling of Cootie watching the moon, because Poppy watched the moon herself sometimes. She liked to imagine moonbabies walking around up there in long, white nighties. What did Cootie imagine when she watched the moon? Maybe she imagined the moon was shining down on her and a whole houseful of friends and they were having a party. Maybe Cootie imagined having her leg back and dancing in the moonlight with all her little statues. Party, Poppy thought, almost rhymed with heart. How did this sound?

Mrs. Kootabelli lived all alone.
In her good heart

She watched the stars and moon
Shine down on her party.

Now it didn't rhyme so well, but she liked the feeling of Mrs. Kootabelli having a party in the moonlight. It was not a perfect poem, but it was a friendly poem. She leaned over and took a sheet of her mother's typing paper from her paperboy bag. She folded it in two, and across the front she wrote neatly with a red ink pen: "To Mrs. Kootabelli." On the inside she wrote the poem and signed "Poppy Field" at the bottom. She looked at the poems written so neatly in red ink on white paper and she imagined how Cootie would feel when she read them. Would she think they were beautiful and full of mystery? Or would she remember Poppy sitting up on the roof, spying on her? If Cootie wanted, she could still lift the curse in time for Neptune Carnival, three weeks from now.

"This better work," she said, hoisting herself out of the lounge chair. She shoved the poems in the paperboy bag and positioned her crutches under her arms. As she stood there she caught a glimpse of Cootie through the hedge. Poppy moved closer and peered in. Cootie was burning again. Poppy sniffed the air for boiled cats, but it was only the sharp, woodsy smell of a campfire. As she watched Cootie stirring the fire around and around with the black poker, she could see her rocking from her good leg to her wooden leg and as she rocked she sang. It sounded like, "Rolla, bolla, bolla, penny a pitch." It was like a chant that a witch would use to turn someone into a bowling ball. Poppy's heart started racing and she moved quickly across the lawn toward the front of the house.

"She *is* crazy," Poppy muttered, as she crutched her way to the mailbox. What if Cootie didn't like the poems and turned Poppy into a bowling ball? Maybe she shouldn't give Cootie the poems after all. But what would Poppy do with the poems if she didn't give them to Cootie? She didn't think anyone would buy them. It would be better to at least have one person read them even if it was an old witch like Cootie. When she got to Cootie's mailbox she took the poems out and looked at them. Then she took out her pen and carefully inked out her name, turning it into a red flower with four petals and a long stem. She did the same on the other poem. Now if Cootie didn't like the poems, she wouldn't know who to put a curse on.

Quickly Poppy looked around. Then she grabbed the rusty latch of the mailbox and yanked the door down and threw in the poems. "There, take them," she said, her heart pounding.

She crutched back alongside the house to the backyard, where she sank down on the lounge chair, exhausted. It was hard work trying to get a curse lifted. She leaned into the chair and draped the blue cloth over her face to think. The silver stars made cool points on her hot, sweaty face. "I'm bushed," she muttered. Bushed was her mother's expression. "I'm a bushed poet with a curse on my head."

Suddenly the blue cloth lifted and there was Tiz, staring down at her. "Is that you, Poppy? I thought it was that crazy old Cootie lying there."

Poppy frowned. "Cootie—what do you mean?"

"You act just like her, hiding under this blue cloth, talking to yourself."

"I was not!" Poppy shouted, snatching back the cloth and pulling it over her face. But she had been talking to herself, she thought, squeezing her eyes shut. Was she starting to act like Cootie?

10

Meaner Than Mud

Today was Poppy's appointment with Dr. Rosenberg. Today he would take off her cast. It was the first thing she thought about when she woke up, her eyes blinking against the sun streaming through the living room drapes. What a relief it would be to go walking out in the sunshine without her crutches, wearing only her comfy old sneakers.

"This is the day," she announced to her mother at breakfast.

"Don't get your hopes up," her mother said, stepping over Poppy's crutches. "Dr. Rosenberg said maybe. You can never count on maybes."

"My leg is perfectly healed," Poppy said. "I can tell, can't I? I mean it is *my* leg. If he took the cast off right this second I could run three miles and never feel a thing. I mean, it wouldn't even hurt."

All the way to the doctor's office, Poppy's heart jumped around like a frog in a box. She looked out the window, watching the kids riding bikes and chasing each other down the sidewalk. Around the corner from Dr. Rosenberg's, two little girls were running through the sprinkler in their swimming suits. Poppy imagined the cold water on her hot, itchy leg.

"I can't wait to go swimming," she told her mother as they pulled into Dr. Rosenberg's parking lot. "I've been doing a lot of visualization lately. I bet I swim better than ever."

"I'll bet you do, too, Sweetheart," her mother said, turning off the car. She leaned over the backseat and looked at Poppy. "It might not be today, Poppy. It might not even be next week. Remember what we talked about."

"I know, I know," Poppy said, reaching for the door handle. In the waiting room, Poppy kept the fingers of both hands crossed for good luck. "Oh please," she said in her mind. "Oh please, oh please, oh please."

When the nurse called "Poppy Field," she was out of her chair in a flash and crutching down the hallway.

"What's this—a crutch race?" Dr. Rosenberg asked, rushing ahead of Poppy to open the door.

"She's just anxious to get her cast off," her mother explained.

"They all are," Dr. Rosenberg said. "And who can blame her? After seven weeks, you're anxious to run around the block and ride your bike again."

"And go swimming," she added.

He grinned. "Right, I forgot that. Well, let's keep our fingers crossed."

Poppy giggled. She thought kids were the

only ones to cross their fingers for luck.

Dr. Rosenberg sent her to X ray, and when he came back in the room, he had the picture of her leg with him. "It looks very good, Poppy."

He showed her where the break had knit together, but Poppy could barely concentrate. He was going to cut off her cast, and she was going to walk out of here on her own leg. She was going to open the car door herself and sit on the front seat like a normal human being. She was going to put her swimming suit on and jump in the lake. She was going to do her Chicken Dance to celebrate. Yes, after dinner she was—

"We're going to cut your cast down today— we'll make a cut out for your knee so you can bend your leg. In another two weeks you should—"

"Two weeks!" Poppy wailed. "Noooo—I want my cast off today."

"I'm sorry, Poppy. You're just not ready. I know you're anxious, but you have the rest of your life to do those things."

"No, I don't," Poppy insisted. "I have to have it off today. I need to swim for Neptune next weekend."

Dr. Rosenberg looked puzzled.

Mrs. Field explained. "It's a big summer party at our beach with all kinds of swimming and diving events. Poppy competes in it every year."

He frowned. "I'm afraid there'll be no swimming races this summer," he said. "You're going to have to take it slow for a while. Even after you get your cast off."

"But I'm perfectly strong," Poppy protested. "It doesn't hurt a bit. Look." She banged her cast up and down against the floor to demonstrate.

"I know," he said. "But we want you to have lots of years of speeding around on this leg. So for this one summer, we're going to slow you down."

Poppy stared glumly at the floor while Dr. Rosenberg cut her cast down to just above her knee. Then he took the saw and cut out a circle where her kneecap was. "That will make your life a lot easier," he said. "Now you can bend your knee.

At the door, Dr. Rosenberg patted her arm. "Now don't be mad at me, Poppy. I only want what's best for you."

But Poppy wasn't mad at Dr. Rosenberg. She was mad at the crazy, mean witch next door. She couldn't believe that after all her poems to Cootie and all her visualization, the curse wasn't lifted in time for Neptune Carnival. "I wish I hadn't written Cootie all those poems," she grumbled on the way home.

"Now, Poppy, I told you she didn't have anything to do with your leg," her mother said. "You just had a bad break and it took longer to heal than we thought. And look on the bright side. Here you are riding beside me instead of being stuck all alone in the backseat." She gave Poppy a quick hug.

"Oh, poo," Poppy said. She reached down and touched her kneecap. What a strange, tickly sensation after all these weeks. Even though it didn't itch, she scratched it with her fingernail, back and forth, watching the pale skin wiggle. "I'm not going to write Cootie any more poems," she said. "I'm not even going to give her the last one I wrote."

"Well, I hope that doesn't mean you're giving up poetry-writing," her mother said. "It's nice having another poet in the family."

"It's a tough business," Poppy said.

"It sure is," her mother agreed.

Even though Poppy was blue about her cast, it gave her a lifted-up feeling to think she shared something with her mother that no one else did.

"I'm going to write a poem about how mad I am at Cootie," Poppy said. "How she let me down."

Her mother smiled. "Well, you're the poet. You can write whatever you want."

"I'm mad," Poppy said.

"I know you are."

When they got home Poppy gathered her notebook and pencils and put them in her paperboy bag and headed for the backdoor. She was surprised at how much lighter her leg felt in its smaller cast. And she liked being able to bend it back and forth. Now she could sit at the table and drink a glass of milk with both legs under her instead of propping her cast on a chair. She looked at her mother. "I'm going outside to write a poem."

"Good luck," her mom said. "I'm going to sit right here and write one."

"Good luck," Poppy said, and stepped out into the sunshine. She noticed that new flowers had come up in her mother's garden to replace the poppies. Now there were daisies and big bushes of pink columbine and tall purple flowers grown from seeds that her father had brought back from Ireland last year. In between the big flowers were little clumps of blue and white forget-me-nots.

She had never noticed how scattered and bright all the colors in the garden were. It reminded her of confetti. She thought of a rhyme: "A boy named Eddie grew flowers like confetti." But she put it out of her mind. She was going to write about mean old Cootie.

She crutched over to her lounge chair and dropped her crutches. Then she pulled off the paperboy bag and sat down. "Mean Old Cootie," she wrote for a title. Pretty soon she wrote: "Old Cootie is meaner than mud." She thought about rhyming words for mud—dud, bud, blood, cud. "She makes me want to drink blood," she wrote. Then she thought about it. Ick. It wasn't true. She never, ever wanted to drink blood. She crossed out the second line and looked over in the direction of Cootie's hedge. What if Cootie could read what she was writing?

"Hey, Pop." Her mom stuck her head out the back door. "I've got to bike over to the library to look something up. Will you be okay for a little bit?"

"What rhymes with mud?" Poppy asked.

"Blood," her mom said. "Bud, cud, crud. See you later."

Poppy waved. Crud—she hadn't thought of crud. Crud was a good word. How about this? "Old Cootie is meaner than mud. As a neighbor she's really a crud." She giggled. Cootie really was a crud. What had she ever done as a neighbor? When she wasn't burning her smelly trash she was hiding inside her old house, thinking up curses, probably. Or talking to her dumb poodle. She looked over the hedge again and saw the billowing smoke. Cootie was out there stirring up her fire and talking to stupid old Stanley right now. Poppy wrote: "Her yard's so full of smoke. She really makes me choke."

Poppy read over her poem and started laughing out loud. After all the nice poems Poppy had written for Cootie, it felt good to write a mean one. It served Cootie right for being such an ugly, scowly old witch. What other terrible things could she put in her poem about Cootie? She glanced over at the dismal gray flag drooping off the flagpole in Cootie's front yard. That terrible flag looked just like a dishrag.

"Wow," Poppy said out loud. It came to her in a flash. "I really hate her flag. It looks like an old dishrag." This was lots of fun. She leaned back in the lounge chair and tapped the pencil against her forehead. As she lay there the smell of smoke was so strong that she pinched her nose. It really was going to make her choke. Only crazy old Cootie would burn her garbage on a hot day like this. And it wasn't exactly a pleasant smell.

Poppy sat up. The smell was getting stronger. Even with her nose plugged she could almost taste the hot, bitter smoke. Now she heard a faint, crackling sound from the other side of the hedge. It was a strange sound, almost like popping corn. She looked up and saw a great puff of dark smoke. Poppy grabbed her crutches and scrambled over to the hedge. What she saw filled her with dread. The blankets on the clothesline had caught fire. Flames danced around the backyard on three sides. And in the center of the ring of fire was Cootie. She had both arms around Stanley and she was staring, open-mouthed, at the flames.

The smoke next to the hedge made Poppy draw back. She wanted to get away from the smoke and the fire as fast she could. But Cootie was in the middle of it and she wasn't moving. Didn't she know there was a fire all around her? Poppy put her hand to her mouth, and yelled, "Run!" But Cootie didn't move. She just stood there with the yellow bow around her neck, like a statue, watching the flames.

"Mom," Poppy yelled. "Mom, come quick." She turned to the back door and then she remembered. Her mother had gone to the library. Tiz and her dad were at work. Just to be certain, she leaned toward the house, and yelled as loud as she could, "Mom! Dad! Tiz!"

Now smoke was pouring through the hedge. Why didn't someone else notice? What could she do all by herself on her stupid broken leg? If she didn't have the dumb cast on, she could jump on her bike and get her mom from the library in three minutes. Or dash across the street to Mrs. Williams' house. Or even run inside and call the fire department. Maybe she should do that anyway. Otherwise Cootie's house was going to catch fire. But she couldn't leave Cootie all alone. She looked at Cootie again. She still hadn't moved. There were big spurts of fire in the grass behind her. "Run, Mrs. Kootabelli," she yelled again. "Run through the hedge." But Cootie just stood there, hugging Stanley and looking frightened.

Poppy was terrified. Now the blanket on the other side of the hedge was on fire. Pretty soon the hedge would catch on fire and Cootie's house, too. She had to get Cootie out of there. "Mrs. Kootabelli, don't be scared. It's me, Poppy," she called. "I'm over here on the other side of the hedge. Please, please, run fast." Even though Cootie couldn't see her through the smoke, Poppy dropped her crutch and put out her hand. "I'm your friend—the one who wrote you the poems. I'm your friend, I'm your friend," she repeated. "You have to get away from the fire. Please!" Cootie turned in the direction of Poppy's voice. She dropped Stanley and looked slowly around.

Poppy waved wildly. "Over here. Hurry. Hurry. Hurry."

The old lady limped forward.

"Hurry!" Poppy yelled. "Keep coming!"

At last Cootie came tottering through the hedge, and Poppy dropped her other crutch and grabbed her and they both fell down.

11

~~~~~~~~~~~~~~~~~~~~~~~~~~~~~~~~~~~~~~

Neptune Princess

It had been a very strange week for Poppy, but the strangest part of it was the moment after Cootie came through the hedge and Poppy grabbed her and they fell down. When they sat up, Cootie was crying. Her little face was all squinched up, and tears were running down her cheeks. Even though she was wrinkled and had gray hair, she made Poppy think of the little girl she had seen at the beach who had lost her mother. She was crying like her heart would break. That's the way Cootie was crying, only more inside herself. Her head bobbed up and down and her shoulders shook, but she didn't make any sound.

Poppy didn't know what to do to make her feel better. So she patted her shoulder. "There, there," she said. As she patted her, she was amazed. How could she ever have been frightened by this poor little lady? Cootie couldn't put a curse on anyone. She couldn't hurt a flea.

She was still patting her shoulder when her mother came around the bend on her bicycle, saw the flames next door, and ran in the house to call the fire department.

The three of them—Mrs. Field, Poppy, and Cootie—sat at the patio table in the backyard and watched the firemen squirt water all over the place.

"Don't worry, Mrs. Kootabelli," her mother said, "your house is going to be fine."

"It's terrible," Cootie said, standing up and craning her neck as if she could see over the hedge. "All my little statues."

"Oh, I'm sorry about them," Mrs. Field said. "Maybe you could get some new ones."

Cootie shook her head. "There was Clarence," she said. "He was a cricket. And there was Stella, the ladybug."

"They must be like little friends," her mother said, patting Cootie's hand.

Cootie pulled a tissue from the box and dabbed at her eyes. "They are my friends," she said. "My only friends."

Poppy couldn't help staring at Cootie, at her thin little body and the droopy yellow ribbon around her neck. This was the closest she had ever been to her. She kept thinking about the little girl who had lost her mother at the beach, and there was no one to take away her scared, lonely feeling. Cootie didn't have a mom or dad. She didn't have a husband or even any children. She lived all alone in that big, old house with no one to talk to or even to argue with. Poppy took a deep breath and repeated what she said to Cootie in the fire, "I'm your friend." Her mother smiled at Poppy and reached over to lift her sweaty bangs off her forehead.

Mrs. Kootabelli didn't say anything. She just dabbed at her eyes. Then she pushed herself out of her chair and stood in front of Poppy. Looking down out of her sad blue eyes, she put out her hands like she wanted to give Poppy a hug. But she just said, "You are a good girl," in her whispery voice. And she patted Poppy's head.

That night everyone in Poppy's family talked about what had happened and how sorry they felt for Mrs. Kootabelli. But most of all, they talked about Poppy.

Tiz said, "Weren't you scared?"

She shook her head. "Not a bit." Then she thought about it. "Yeah, a little. For a second I wanted to run away."

Her father put his arm around her. "I don't know many ten-year-olds levelheaded enough to help Mrs. Kootabelli. You know, Poppy, when I'm away I think of you as my little whirling dervish, but when I come back I find that you're very grown up." Then he added, "Sometimes you amaze me."

"I do?" Poppy felt her heart swell with pride. She snuggled under her father's arm and thought about what a grown-up and level-headed person she was.

But before she went to sleep that night she thought about Cootie again. She took the poem she had written out of her paperboy bag. "Mean Old Cootie," she read.

"Old Cootie is meaner than mud.
As a neighbor she's really a crud.
Her yard's so full of smoke,
She makes everyone choke.
I just hate her flag.
It looks like an old dishrag."

Poppy was so ashamed of what she had written that she tore it up and dropped the pieces in the duck wastebasket. Then she lay down and thought about Cootie until she fell asleep.

The next day after work, Tiz and Mr. Field

went over and cleaned up Cootie's backyard. They pulled up all the little melted statues and threw them in the trash, and they picked up pieces of old burned blanket that lay scattered around the yard like hunks of wet, black fur. Then they raked up all the leaves and ribbons and scraps of paper and garbage from under the hedge and around the barbecue pit. At the end of the day they dragged away seven garbage bags full of stuff.

"What a dump," Tiz said. "We even tossed out that half-baked blue poodle she used to drag around. It was burnt to a crisp."

Poppy's heart sank. How Cootie would miss poor Stanley.

"Maybe to you it was a dump," Mrs. Field said, "but Mrs. Kootabelli thought it was beautiful—full of leaves and little statues that she loved."

"And garbage and litter," Tiz added.

"Now I want you to take this hamburger casserole over to her," Mrs. Field said. "I suspect the poor little thing doesn't eat very well."

All week long the Fields did little kindnesses

for Cootie. Mr. Field replaced a window that had been cracked by the fire, and Mrs. Field sent over a kettle of chicken vegetable soup.

"I want to be friends with Mrs. Kootabelli, but she's not the friendly type," Poppy complained. "She doesn't even come into her backyard anymore."

"She's very shy," Mrs. Field said. "She's a little afraid of people, I think."

Poppy laughed. "Who could be afraid of us?" But then she remembered how afraid she had been of Cootie.

The Saturday of Neptune Carnival arrived. Poppy looked at the bright sunshine slipping through the living room drapes and it made her think of Cootie's yellow ribbon. She sighed and sat up. She almost wished it would be gray and rainy, the way it sometimes was for the carnival.

"Where's my swimsuit, Poppy?"

Poppy glared at Tiz. "What are you asking me for? Do I look like Mom?"

Tiz was swimming even if Poppy wasn't, and

they were all going down to the beach. But she wanted her parents to say, "There's no reason to go down if Poppy isn't swimming. She's the only person we really want to watch. Let's just drive into town and go to a horror movie instead."

But when Poppy hobbled into the kitchen, her dad said, "Come on, Poppy. Let's move it. We don't want to miss any of the action." He pushed her back toward the living room. "Just get dressed. We can buy some juice and doughnuts down there."

"I found my swimsuit," Tiz said, running back through the living room and tossing it in the air.

"Big deal," Poppy grumbled, putting on her left tennis shoe.

"You ready?" her mom asked, passing through with her sunglasses and some sunscreen. "Here, let's put some of this on you. We'll be down there for a while."

"How—" Poppy didn't finish. She had to press her lips together to keep the coconutty lotion from running into her mouth.

"I asked Mrs. Kootabelli to come with us," Mrs. Field said as they were getting into the car.

Everyone stopped and looked over at Cootie's front door.

"But she said no," Mrs. Field added.

"Natch," said Tiz. "You couldn't get that old bat out of there for a million bucks."

"She's not an old bat," Poppy snapped, wishing *she* had thought of asking Cootie. She had told Cootie she was her friend, but she hadn't even seen her since the fire. "You're the bat," she said to Tiz. "I don't see how you can expect to swim when you can't see two feet without your glasses."

"My, we're a little testy, aren't we?" Tiz said. "Could we be a little jealous, Missed Neptune Princess?" Tiz slapped his knee. "Get it? She missed being Neptune Princess."

Poppy glared at Tiz as they got out of the car. She hoped he got tangled in the lane ropes and had to be rescued. Tiz was the worst swimmer at the beach. He had never once won a single blue ribbon.

As they walked around talking to people and munching doughnuts, Poppy looked at the big, blue winner's platform in the middle of the beach. They put it up every year and decorated it with hundreds of little plastic pennants in all colors. She listened to the pennants slapping against each other in the breeze and thought about how many times she had stood on the platform and listened to that sound. It was like people clapping. She sighed and leaned on her crutches to rest.

"Not this year, huh?" It was Mr. Hoban, the editor of the *McGregor Beach Weekly*.

Poppy smiled and shook her head.

"Well, there'll be other years for a fine swimmer like you," he said, patting her shoulder.

"Thank you," Poppy said, but she didn't feel very thankful. She crutched off to look for Kim and Marcie. They were in their swimsuits under the lifeguard stand. To avoid the sand she had to crutch the long way around, on the grass at the edge of the shore. By the time she got to them, Mr. Hoban had started his announcements. "Ladies and gentlemen—"

"Hi, you guys," Poppy said. "Are you in the first event?"

"Ssssh," Kim said, trying to hear.

"Welcome to the thirty-fifth annual—"

"Boring," Marcie said. She squeezed Poppy's arm. "Hey, sorry you didn't get your cast off."

"Yeah," Poppy said, slumping down on her crutches.

"Before we begin, there's a little something—" Mr. Hoban went on.

"Where's your mom and dad?" Marcie asked.

"Over there." Poppy pointed at a bunch of adults in bright shorts who were waving their arms at each other and shrieking with laughter like little kids. She and Marcie rolled their eyes at each other.

"—sent to me by a lady in the subdivision. Someone we don't hear from much. I'd like you all to hear it. It concerns—"

"Hey!" Kim poked Poppy's arm. "He said your name."

Poppy looked up at Mr. Hoban, who was looking down at a piece of paper in his hand. Everyone else was looking at her. "What did he say?" she whispered.

"Sssh," Marcie said.

"Dear Mr. Editor," he read,

"Maybe you heard that there was a terrible fire in my backyard. I was in the middle of that fire and I didn't know which way to turn. If you have ever been in the middle of a fire, you know what I mean. I just thought I was going to burn up in that fire. And good-bye to the world. And then I heard a little voice. It was the sweetest little voice in the world. It was Poppy Field calling to me, calling, 'Hurry over to me. Follow my voice and you will be safe.' She said it over and over. 'I am your friend,' she said. 'Follow my voice.' And I did. I followed her little

138

voice and I was safe. This is to let you know that Poppy Field is a good friend for an old lady to have. I will never forget her little voice calling to me. Yours truly, Mrs. Kootabelli."

Poppy's mouth dropped open. It was as if Cootie had given her the warmest hug of her life.

"Wow." Marcie and Kim stared at her.

Poppy could feel everyone else staring at her, too. She felt her face get bright red.

"Yaa-aa-y, Poppy." It was Tiz yelling at her from the other side of the beach.

"Yay, Poppy," someone else said, and started clapping. All of a sudden everyone started clapping. Kim and Marcie and the Burkes and the Williams and Tina and all the kids and all the adults. They put down their cups of coffee and lemonade and all clapped. She looked over to where her parents had been standing and they were looking back at her. But they weren't clapping. They had their arms around each other, and they were just looking at her and smiling and smiling as if she were the only person on the whole beach.

But Poppy was glad she wasn't the only person on the beach. She was surrounded by all her friends and family. And by Cootie. Poppy smiled back at them all until she thought her face would break.